WHEN I GOT WITHIN A BLOCK OF MY HOUSE, I STARTED TO RUN.

No Help ran after me. I knew he could catch up to me if he wanted to, but he stayed about fifteen feet back.

When I got to my house he waited on the sidewalk, watching while I opened my front door and went inside. I was glad I had remembered to take my key that day so that I didn't have to get the spare one from under the fake rock where we hid it.

I locked the front door behind me, then ran to the window and peered out. No Help had turned and was walking back toward the bus stop.

Why had he followed me home? The only possible answer was that he wanted to scare me, to warn me not to tell anyone what I had seen.

BOOKS BY PEG KEHRET

PEG KEHRET

DANGEROUS DECEPTION

PUFFIN BOOKS

PUFFIN BOOKS
An imprint of Penguin Random House LLC
375 Hudson Street
New York, New York 10014

First published in the United States of America by Dutton Children's Books,
an imprint of Penguin Group (USA) LLC, 2014
Published by Puffin Books, an imprint of Penguin Random House LLC, 2015

THE LIBRARY OF CONGRESS HAS CATALOGED THE DUTTON CHILDREN'S BOOKS EDITION AS FOLLOWS:
Kehret, Peg.
Dangerous deception / by Peg Kehret.
pages cm.
Summary: Sixth-grader Emmy and her classmates start a secret community service project to help a hungry family,
but soon Emmy finds herself involved in a home burglary ring operated by the family's neighbor.
ISBN 978-0-525-42652-3 (hardcover)
[1. Charity—Fiction. 2. Burglary—Fiction. 3. Service learning–Fiction. 4. Schools—Fiction.
5. Family life—Fiction. 6. Kidnapping—Fiction.] I. Title.
PZ7.K2518Dap 2014
[Fic]—dc23   2013049856

Puffin Books ISBN 978-0-14-751175-1

Printed in the United States of America

1 3 5 7 9 10 8 6 4 2

For Seth Robert
August 10, 2011

DANGEROUS DECEPTION

CHAPTER ONE

only intended to help two children who were hungry and had no money for food. That's an admirable goal for a sixth-grade girl, isn't it? You can't get in trouble for doing unto others as you would have them do unto you. Right?

Wrong! I may have had noble intentions, but I still ended up causing a car crash, being abducted by a thug, and smuggling a scared cat on a city bus by sticking him inside my T-shirt, a maneuver I do not recommend unless you're wearing a steel undershirt.

I wasn't.

It all began when Mom got sick. I know it wasn't her fault. Nobody would choose to spend half the day moaning in bed and the other half dashing to the bathroom. Still, it was a terrible time for her to get the flu. I suppose there isn't a good time to have the flu, but Mom is especially busy in April.

She works in the children's department at Dunbar's, the biggest department store in Cedar Hill. Every April Dunbar's has a big contest, "Make Your Dunbar's Dream Come True." The entry forms look like this:

If I could have anything I want from Dunbar's Department Store, I would choose…
Finish the sentence in one hundred words or less, telling what you want and why. Then bring your completed entry to Dunbar's and drop it in the big red Dunbar's Dream box on the second floor or mail it to the address below.
One lucky winner will have his/her Dunbar's Dream come true.
Two runners-up each receive a $25.00 gift card.

There's a place for the person's name, address, and phone number, and then in small print, it says, "All entries are confidential. Contestants must be eighteen or older." That's followed by Dunbar's mailing address.

The first year that Dunbar's had the contest, April sales increased by 35 percent. Apparently, people looked at all the merchandise to decide what they wanted most and then ended up buying it when they didn't win. Naturally there is now a Dunbar's Dream Contest every year.

Since the big red box where people leave their contest entries is in Dunbar's children's department, Mom was asked to empty it each evening and go through the entries to choose the best ones. The top ten get passed along to Dunbar's manager, Mrs. Murphy, who selects the winner.

The first year, Mom volunteered her time. By the second year, the number of contest entries increased so much that Dunbar's agreed to pay her extra for judging the contest. At that time, she also promised in writing not to tell anyone that she was a judge or to share the contents of the entries with anyone other than Mrs. Murphy.

The day she got the flu was the first week of this year's Dunbar's Dream Contest. Piles of entries covered our dining room table. I'd had to eat breakfast standing at the kitchen counter, which made me cranky, and I was even crankier when I got home from school. It had been a rotten day.

Somewhere between leaving home that morning and arriving in my third-period history class, I had lost the history homework that I'd done the night before. I found it later, tucked inside my library book, but by then third period was over, so even though I turned in my assignment, I got an automatic grade deduction for being late.

Then it was Cook's Surprise Day in the school cafeteria, which meant I had Gag Casserole for lunch. No sane person wants to make this, but in case you are curious, here is the recipe:

GAG CASSEROLE RECIPE
Mix cooked macaroni in a lumpy white sauce with leftover peas, carrots, corn, and whatever else you can find from the day before. (Sometimes called Clean-out-the-Fridge

Casserole.) Bake until heated through. Drop globs onto
plates. To lessen chance of gagging, hold nose while eating.

Some kids swear the cook actually puts table scraps from kids' plates into a big bowl and then stirs it all together to make Gag Casserole. I don't believe that, but I always bring a sandwich on Cook's Surprise Day. Not this time. Mom's the one who remembers to check the school menus and make me a lunch if the entrée isn't something I like, but that morning she didn't get up because she wasn't feeling well. She was in bed when I left and still in bed when I got home.

Her voice sounded quavery when I let myself in. "Is that you, Emmy?"

I stood in the doorway of her bedroom. "How are you feeling?" I asked.

"Awful."

"Did you go to work for a while?"

Mom shook her head. "I didn't even get dressed."

"How did you get more contest entries? There's a whole new bag of them on the table."

"Colleen dropped them off. She worked for me today."

"Did it not occur to her that, since you have the flu, she could offer to read the entries this time, or pass them along to Mrs. Murphy?"

"Colleen's only worked there a couple of months," she said. "She probably doesn't realize how much time the contest takes."

Waggy, our goofy black Lab mix, stood by the door making the little woof sounds that he makes when he needs to go out, so I snapped the leash on him and took him for a quick walk. Yes, I know that Waggy is not a particularly clever name for a dog, but I was only six when we adopted him. At least I didn't call him Blackie.

When I returned, I fixed Mom a cup of tea and a slice of toast, but the sight of food made her more nauseated than she already was and she bolted for the bathroom. I gave the crusts to Waggy, ate the rest of the toast myself, and watered our houseplants with the tea.

"How did your day go?" Mom asked, after she staggered back to bed.

I rolled my eyes. "We have to do a community service project," I said, "and I'm in the same group with Jelly Bean Logan and Shoeless Parsh. They spent most of our allotted time arguing that we could go to Dairy Queen after school and have it count as a project for feeding the hungry. I'm in the worst group of the whole class."

"Is it only the three of you?"

"No," I said. "Lauren and Abby are in my group, too. So is Hunter Kramer."

"Then the four of you can outvote Jelly Bean and Shoeless," Mom said.

"They are such blockheads," I said.

"How did Shoeless get that ridiculous nickname?" Mom asked.

"He stomped in mud during recess on his first day of kindergarten, and the teacher made him leave his shoes off for the rest of the day."

"Kindergarten was six years ago."

"He's every bit as wacky now as he was then," I said. "His only talent is to wiggle both ears at the same time. They go up and down really fast."

Mom closed her eyes, as if she couldn't bear to hear another word about Shoeless. I can't say that I blame her.

"I guess I'm on my own for dinner," I said.

"Yes."

If Dad had been here, I would have lobbied to have pizza delivered, but Dad was in Alaska for two weeks. He installs and maintains complicated computer programs in hospital pharmacies and teaches the hospital personnel how to use them. He's often away for a week or more at a time.

I knew there was no point asking if I could order pizza. For the last six months, Mom's been on a mission to encourage me to lose weight. She's never actually said she thinks I'm too fat, but she constantly reads food labels out loud, especially the calorie count and the grams of sugar and fat. I hate it when she does that.

The thing is, I know I weigh more than I should. I know my thighs are flabby and my butt's too big. I don't need Mom or anybody else to point it out to me. I can see myself in the mirror and, one of these days, I plan to get in shape, but I'll do it when I decide I want to, not because somebody else doesn't like the way I look. I wish the media would quit telling us about the obesity epidemic of America's children. I am not obese, but because of all the hype, my parents are afraid I will be.

I poured a glass of orange juice, then picked the broccoli out of some leftover mac-and-cheese before I zapped it. Mom tries to sneak broccoli into everything, claiming that the taste of the mac-and-cheese or spaghetti or whatever else she's contaminating will overpower the taste of broccoli. It doesn't work. Luckily for me, Waggy likes broccoli.

I pushed some of the contest entries aside to make room for my plate.

While I ate I started reading the entries. The first one said, "I would choose a dishwasher because it would save me a lot of time. My lazy husband never helps with the dishes, and I end up spending half the night cleaning up the kitchen while he watches TV. What I really need is a new husband, but a dishwasher would help a lot."

The second entrant was a girl named Allison. I could tell by the handwriting that she was a kid, even though the contest rules state you have to be eighteen or older. Allison said she would choose a Barbie and a makeup kit. I was tempted to send her a letter, since her address was on the entry form.

Dear Allison:
   Barbies and makeup kits are fine, but why not
ask for a microscope, too, or a basketball? Let's not
limit ourselves here, girl.

Of course I couldn't do that so I read the next entry in the pile. Then I read it again.

   I would choose food, any kind. My little
sister, Trudy, cries in her bed at night because she's

hungry. I take an empty sack to school every day
and pretend to have a lunch. All of Mama's pay this
month went for our rent. She will find a second job
as soon as she gets well. We need cat food, too. My
cat is hungry.

The entry was signed *Sophie*. No last name. She lived at
1135 East Sycamore, Apt. 3.

Dunbar's doesn't have a grocery section, but there is
a small coffee stand just inside the main entrance that sells
pastries and a few pre-packaged sandwiches, in addition to
specialty coffee drinks. Maybe Sophie hoped to win tuna-salad
sandwiches and lemon pound cake.

I thought about the people who had won the Dunbar's
Dream Contest in the previous six years. One got a dining
room set. Another received an upright freezer. Nearly all of the
entrants chose expensive items, such as appliances or furniture.

You don't need a dining room set or a freezer if you have no
food. Sophie needed bread and apples and cans of soup. She and
her sister needed bananas and oatmeal and peanut butter. Feeling
guilty, I realized they'd probably even be glad to get broccoli.

Thinking about all that food made me hungry, so I took
the package of shortbread cookies out of my backpack and
opened it. Mom had quit keeping any kind of dessert in the
house, so I was forced to spend my own money on treats.
Usually I stopped at the mini-mart after school, even though
the prices there were higher than at the supermarket.

By evening, Mom felt better. I took her some apple juice

and while she sipped it, I said, "I read a few of the contest entries. There's one from a girl who says her family needs food."

"Some of those entries break my heart," Mom said.

"You mean you've had entries like that before, from needy kids who don't have enough to eat?"

"Not from kids. But there are plenty of people in Cedar Hill who can't afford warm clothes or beds."

"When you get entries like that, what do you do?"

"In prior years the Help Your Neighbor organization contacted the person and offered to supply what they needed, but this year their donations are way down. They've already used most of this year's budget."

"Then who helps people like Sophie? Will you and Dad buy food for her family?"

"I wish I could help, but I can't."

"Why not?" We aren't wealthy, but I knew Mom and Dad contributed to several charitable organizations. I couldn't imagine why she would not help kids who need food so badly that they enter a contest to get it.

"Dunbar's won't let me."

"What? Why would anyone care if you helped a hungry child?"

"It has to do with Dunbar's privacy policy. Dunbar's can give someone's name to a registered nonprofit organization such as Help Your Neighbor, but they can't give it to individuals. The first year that I read the contest entries, one asked for shoes for her little boy. She said her son's only shoes were too small, so she had cut the toes out and now the kids at school made fun of him. Out of all the merchandise in Dunbar's what that woman wanted most was shoes for her little boy."

"So, did Help Your Neighbor give him new shoes?"

"Help Your Neighbor was not yet involved, so I showed the letter to Mrs. Murphy and told her I planned to mail that woman a gift card to use for shoes."

"Good idea."

"I didn't do it, though. Mrs. Murphy reminded me that I had signed a confidentiality agreement when Dunbar's hired me, agreeing that I would not disclose any Dunbar's business to anyone other than my supervisor. I'm already bending the rules by discussing the entries with you; giving gifts to people who entered the contest would be cause for my dismissal."

"That's ridiculous!" I said. "Why would they fire you for helping a little boy get a pair of shoes?"

"Dunbar's states in the contest rules that what the entrants ask for will be kept secret. I didn't push the matter because I feared if I made a fuss about it, the higher-ups would decide I couldn't help with the contests. I enjoy screening the entries, and the extra money has been nice."

"Doesn't it break the confidentiality agreement to tell Help Your Neighbor about some of the requests?"

"Their attorney drew up an agreement with Help Your Neighbor. They never mention Dunbar's contest. They contact people as part of a random survey and then discover what the people need. Now that they've almost run out of funds, I don't know what will happen."

In bed that night, I thought about Sophie's contest entry. I often complained at bedtime that I was starving and had to have hot chocolate or popcorn before I could fall asleep, but I had never actually gone to bed hungry. I thought of little Trudy crying from hunger pangs. I stroked Waggy, who was stretched out beside me, and thought how awful it would be to have no food for a hungry pet. I had to help Sophie, no matter what Dunbar's privacy rules said.

I got up, retrieved Sophie's entry, and stuck it in my backpack. My group at school needed a community service project. Maybe I had found it.

Mom could lose her job if she personally helped someone who entered the contest, but Dunbar's couldn't fire me or my classmates. Mom didn't give me the letter. If I don't tell her what I'm doing, she won't be in trouble.

CHAPTER TWO

Right after lunch the next day, Mrs. Reed had us divide into our community service groups. "In half an hour," she said, "I want each group to submit their first choice for a project."

Crystal Warren said, "There's going to be a new TV show called *The Biggest Helpers*, about kids who do service projects. The group with the best project wins a million dollars!"

We all looked at Crystal but said nothing. Crystal often announces "news" that she swears came from reliable sources but are really the ridiculous headlines on tabloid newspapers, or maybe just stuff she makes up. The rest of us had learned long ago not to pay any attention to Crystal.

"Get into your groups, please," Mrs. Reed said.

Jelly Bean and Shoeless picked up right where they had left off the day before.

"First choice," said Shoeless, "is an after-school pizza party for the hungriest group in Cedar Hill. Us."

"Second choice," said Jelly Bean, "would be if we go to Dairy Queen instead of getting pizza."

"We are not doing any project that feeds us," Lauren said.

"This is supposed to be something to benefit the community," Abby said.

"There are kids in Cedar Hill who are really hungry," I said. "They are the ones we need to help."

"I'm really hungry," said Shoeless. He wiggled his ears up and down, as if that would prove how emaciated he was.

"So am I," said Jelly Bean. "If a Hunger Meter could measure how empty my stomach is, I would hold the world's record."

"Give me a break," said Abby.

"You guys are lame," said Hunter.

"Yeah?" said Jelly Bean. "Well, let's hear one of you come up with a good community service project."

"I have one," I said as I took Sophie's contest entry out of my backpack, "but before I tell you what it is, you have to promise to keep it a secret."

"We're going undercover for a drug sting!" said Shoeless. "Hoo-ha! I've always wanted to be a plainclothes detective."

"It isn't a drug sting," I said.

"If it's your idea, it must involve chocolate," said Hunter. "I saw you eat three cupcakes at lunch yesterday."

"I forgot to bring a lunch, and I didn't want to get sick

from eating Gag Casserole," I said. I wanted to add that what I eat is none of his business, but I didn't.

"So, what's the project?" asked Jelly Bean.

"You won't tell anyone?"

Curiosity prompted them all to agree to keep the secret, so I read Sophie's entry out loud. For once, Shoeless and Jelly Bean had no smart remarks.

"Wow," Abby said. "That girl sounds desperate."

"Her little sister cries herself to sleep because she's so hungry," Hunter said, as if he had to say it out loud in order to believe it.

"This project will be simple," said Jelly Bean. "All we have to do is mail the entry to one of the TV stations. They'll read it on the air and a couple of hundred people will send a bunch of food and money. Problem solved."

"That would work, except for one thing," I said. "As I said, the contest entry has to remain a secret. We can't tell anyone about it."

"What's the big deal about keeping quiet?" Shoeless asked. "This is one of those stories that TV announcers love. It's a tearjerker when they read it on the air, and then two days later they can say what generous viewers they have, and take credit for solving Sophie's problem."

"It's against the contest rules for Dunbar's to show the entries to anyone else," I said. "If we go public with this, my mom gets fired."

"We have a major problem," said Hunter.

Mrs. Reed interrupted by announcing, "You have five

more minutes to decide on your first choice for a project."

"We can't tell her, either," I said.

"Why not?" said Abby. "We could show her Sophie's entry, and explain why we have to keep it secret, and ask if we can have a food drive. We can call it something generic like 'Food for Hungry Children' so that Mrs. Reed is the only one besides our group who knows where the food will go."

"That might work," I said, wishing I'd thought of it myself.

"Let's try it," said Lauren.

"Yes," said Hunter. "The worst that can happen is she'll say no and then we'll have to think of a different community service project."

"There's always Dairy Queen or pizza," said Shoeless.

Abby said, "I move that we show the letter to Mrs. Reed and explain why we can't tell anyone else."

"Since I am a totally unselfish person who always puts others first," said Jelly Bean, "I vote yes."

"Even though I am seriously malnourished myself," said Shoeless, "I vote yes."

"Oh, brother," said Lauren.

It was unanimous, and the group chose me to present our proposal to Mrs. Reed.

The other groups from my class all gave their proposals orally. Their spokesperson simply stood and explained what the group wanted to do. When my turn came, I said, "My group needs to present a written proposal."

"Oh?" said Mrs. Reed. "Why is that?" I think she suspected that we weren't ready and were trying to buy extra time, but I had been writing down our proposed project while the other groups presented their ideas.

I held up my paper and Sophie's contest entry. "If you read our proposal, I think you'll understand," I said.

Mrs. Reed looked unconvinced, but she took the two papers. She read my group's proposal first, in which I explained about Dunbar's rules and how Mom could lose her job. I could see her expression change as she read what Sophie had written. When she had finished reading, she said, "Your proposal is approved. Please stay in for a few minutes during afternoon recess so that I can talk to you about it."

I looked at Lauren, Abby, and Hunter. They were grinning at me. Jelly Bean and Shoeless high-fived each other. Our project was approved. Now all we had to do was figure out how to make it work.

When the other kids left for recess, my group hovered around Mrs. Reed's desk.

"This will not be an official class project if we can't talk about it in class," she said, "but I am willing to give you credit for it, anyway. However, you will need to tell your mother what you are doing, Emmy."

I gulped. "I can't do that," I said. "If she knew, then she would make us stop."

"I do not condone hiding your actions from your parents," she said. "What if the secret gets out? What if someone at Dunbar's finds out what you're doing?"

"If that happens," I said, "I want to be able to say that Mom didn't know anything about it. I can say she told me at the start that I couldn't help Sophie, and she had no idea that I had gone ahead."

Mrs. Reed sighed. "In this case," she said, "perhaps it is better if your parents don't know what you're doing. For that matter, it would be better if I didn't know what you are doing, either, so from here on, you are on your own and if anyone asks if this is a school project, the answer is no."

We all stared at her. "Your mother is not the only one who could get in trouble for breaking the rules," she said. "You may go to recess now."

We all trooped out to the playground but none of us felt like playing kickball or scaling the new rock-climbing wall. Instead we clumped together by the drinking fountain and considered our next move.

"Instead of having a big school-wide food drive," I said, "we'll each have to collect donations on our own."

"I can ask my grandma," Abby said.

"My neighbors are good about supporting whatever I'm involved in," said Hunter.

"Collecting food won't be the only hard part," I said. "We also have to deliver it to Sophie's house. I looked up her address, and she lives on the east side of Cedar Hill, over by the gravel pit."

Our school sat on the western edge of town and, since it was a neighborhood school, my classmates and I all lived on the west side.

"That's way too far to walk," Lauren said, "especially if we're carrying bags of groceries."

"My brother got his driver's license last week," Jelly Bean said. "He's always looking for an excuse to drive the car. If I tell my parents I have a load of stuff to take to school for an assignment, they'll let Chance drive me tomorrow and then, after school, he can take all the food to Sophie's house."

"Can we trust Chance to keep quiet about it?" I asked.

"He never tells our parents anything," Jelly Bean said, "and there would be no reason to tell his buddies. They're high-and-mighty juniors who don't believe it's possible that sixth graders would do anything of interest to them."

By the time recess ended we had a plan. Each of us would try to collect one grocery bag full of food items after school that day. We'd bring our bags to school the next morning, and Jelly Bean would arrange for his brother to pick him up after school. We'd load all our food into Chance's car, and Jelly Bean and I would ride along to deliver it to Sophie's house. Chance would drive me home afterward.

"Then what?" said Lauren.

"Tomorrow night I'll write up a report for Mrs. Reed, with a copy for each of you," I said. I felt satisfied and efficient. We were going to help a girl who really needed assistance, and fulfill our community service assignment at the same time.

"I mean what happens to Sophie after tomorrow?" Lauren said. "The food we collect will probably last only a week or two and then she'll be right back in the same predicament she's in now. We need to find a more permanent solution."

My satisfaction leaked away. Lauren was right. Our plan

for tomorrow was a good one, but it was like pumping air into a bike tire without fixing the leak. Sophie's family might require help for many weeks, and I couldn't think of any way to make that happen.

"I wonder if Sophie knows about the food bank," Hunter said. "Her family could get groceries there."

"She might not have transportation to go there, or a way to carry the food home," said Shoeless.

"Maybe we should go to the food bank," Abby said. "We can talk to someone there and tell them we know of a family who needs help. We can ask what to do."

"Does anyone know where the food bank is?" I asked.

Heads shook.

"I'll find out," Lauren offered. "I'll learn where it is and when it's open and how it works."

On the way home from school, I worried about what would happen if our plan wasn't kept secret. Besides me, five people in my group, plus Mrs. Reed, knew what we were doing. Soon Jelly Bean's brother would know, too. It would take only one slip of the tongue as someone asked for a donation of food and our project would be uncovered. If that happened, then what? What about Mom's job? How much trouble would I be in? Rain trickled down the bus windows, making the view as dreary as my mood.

I had felt fairly confident that we could pull this off when it was a school food drive; doing it on our own was more complicated. If the food bank didn't work out for Sophie's family, we would need to collect more food later, but I couldn't ask my neighbors over and over.

How would we know if Sophie's family was okay or if they needed more help? Perhaps instead of leaving the food anonymously I should tell Sophie who I am and how to contact me. But what if her mom called my house and my mom answered? Our community service project hadn't even started yet and we already had problems.

When I got home, I pushed my concerns aside. My grandma always says to do what needs to be done today and let tomorrow worry about itself. I found a big cloth tote bag to hold the food I collected. Luckily, Mom had felt well enough to return to work that morning so I didn't have to explain my actions.

Whenever I have to sell stuff for school, Mom and Dad always insist that I go with a friend, rather than knocking on doors by myself. This time I was alone, so I went only to the homes of neighbors I know. That way, I'd be safe.

By the time I left on my mission, the April showers had stopped and the dark clouds had moved on, replaced by sky the color of a first-place ribbon. My mood brightened, too. I'm doing a good thing, I told myself. I'm helping someone who is less fortunate, so how can that lead to trouble?

I decided to go to the houses at the far end of my block first, and work my way home so I wouldn't have to carry the food both directions.

I skipped Mrs. Braider, who lives next door to me. Even

though I was certain Mrs. Braider would contribute, I also knew I could count on her to say something to Mom about it. Mrs. Braider is one of those gossipy people who spends her time poking her nose into other people's business.

When I was three, Mom had turned the hose to a slight drizzle on a hot summer day and allowed me to water the flowers in our backyard. I had a wonderful time until Mrs. Braider called Mom to report that I was wasting water by sprinkling the fence instead of the roses, and Mom told me to stop. After that, I had thought of our neighbor as Big Mouth Braider.

In the years since then, the trees and shrubs in our backyard had grown thick and tall, blocking off her view. Now she could spy on us only when we were out in front.

I hurried past her house with my empty tote bag, and then again when I returned with the bag loaded with food items.

When I told my neighbors that my class was collecting food for a needy family, they generously handed over cans of soup, baked beans, evaporated milk, and spaghetti sauce. I received a box of oatmeal, packets of hot chocolate mix, two kinds of crackers, macaroni-and-cheese mix, and even a big tin of fancy mixed nuts, the expensive kind with lots of cashews.

The nuts came from Mrs. Woodburn, who lives with a parrot named Popeye.

"Go away!" squawked Popeye, when I rang the doorbell. "Go away!"

"Hush, Popeye," said Mrs. Woodburn as she tried to hear what I wanted.

When she handed me the nuts, she said, "These were a birthday gift, but I'm on a diet. You're doing me a big favor by taking away temptation."

"Thanks," I said. "I'm sure this will be a treat."

"Go away!" shrieked Popeye. He ruffled his bright green feathers, as if he wanted to fly toward me.

I wondered how Mrs. Woodburn could stand the screeching, but as I left she leaned close to Popeye's cage and said, "Kiss, kiss!" Popeye stretched forward, put his thick yellow beak near her lips, and I swear he said, "Kiss, kiss," too.

When I got to the Freemans' home, Mr. Freeman asked me to step inside so he could close the door. "We don't want the cats to get out," he explained. "Bieber and Gaga are regular escape artists. We should have named them both Houdini." As if to prove his point, two black-and-white cats dashed toward the fresh air. When the door shut before they got to it, they rubbed on my ankles and waved their tails back and forth.

The cats reminded me of Sophie's request.

"I'm collecting cat food as well as people food," I said. "The family who will be getting this donation has a pet cat."

"Did you hear that, Martha?" Mr. Freeman called to his wife, who had gone into the kitchen. "The family that Emmy is helping needs cat food."

Mrs. Freeman returned with several cans of cat food, a big jar of three-bean salad, two cans of peaches, and a gray felt catnip mouse with a tail and whiskers.

I laughed when I saw the mouse. "This is perfect," I said. "Thank you so much."

"It's always nice to see young people doing an unselfish deed," Mrs. Freeman said. "Your parents must be proud of you."

Her comment shot holes in my good mood because as soon as she said it, I realized that by talking to my neighbors I had added a whole lot more people who knew what I was doing. My community service team might as well open a Facebook page and announce ourselves to the world. Even without Mrs. Braider, it would be a miracle if Mom and Dad didn't learn that I had asked my neighbors to donate food for a needy family.

In less than an hour my bag was full, and so heavy I could hardly lift it. It would be a challenge to carry it to the school bus tomorrow, but I couldn't ask Mom to drive me. She'd want to know what I had in the bag.

Back home, I found a second tote bag and divided the load, to make it easier to carry. I also wrote a note which I put in one of the bags. "For Sophie and her family from a secret friend." I smiled as I imagined Sophie reading it.

The next morning, I counted on Mom not paying much attention to me. She's usually distracted in the mornings, getting herself ready to leave for work. I ate my breakfast slowly. I planned to wait until it was time to leave for the bus, and then slip into my room, get the two bags, and hurry out the door.

When I heard the hair dryer turn on in the bathroom, I hollered, "Bye, Mom. I'm leaving!"

"Love you," she called.

"Love you, too!" I grabbed the groceries, and was on my way.

I lugged the tote bags up the steps of the bus and stopped next to Lauren. Usually we sit together, but the seat beside her held a big brown paper bag full of food. She lifted it onto her lap to make room for me. I put one tote bag on the floor between my feet and held the other one.

"Looks like you collected a lot," Lauren said.

"So did you."

"I could have gotten even more," Lauren said, "but I didn't have any way to get it to school. If we collect food again, I have plenty more neighbors I can ask."

Hunter met Lauren and me at the door of our classroom. "Mrs. Reed said to put your bags of food in the supply closet," he said.

Abby brought a cardboard box with the tops of cans, boxes, and bottles of catsup and salad dressing sticking up like a city skyline. Soon Shoeless and Jelly Bean arrived. They each had two bags of food, too. I hadn't been sure they would actually follow through. Shoeless consistently avoided his homework, and Jelly Bean had a million excuses for not doing what he was supposed to do. This time, they surprised me.

"Chance has the car," Jelly Bean said. "He drove me to school, and he'll deliver all the food for us after school."

The rest of the day dragged. Thoughts of Sophie's little sister filled my mind. Trudy was hungry, and we had a whole lot of food for her. It seemed too bad that she had to wait until three o'clock to get it.

CHAPTER THREE

At recess, Lauren said, "I Googled the Cedar Hill food bank last night. It's in the main room of the Community Center, every Tuesday, Thursday, and Saturday from ten until two."

"Did it say what you have to do to receive food?" Abby asked. "Do you have to somehow prove that you qualify as low-income or can anyone show up and get free food?"

"It didn't say," Lauren said.

"I'll find out," Shoeless said. "I'll go there Saturday morning and ask for something to eat, and if they give it to me we'll know you don't have to fill out paperwork."

"They probably don't hand out food to kids," Lauren said.

"Why not?" Shoeless said. "Kids get hungry. We got started on this project because of Sophie and Trudy. I'll say I'm representing a community service project for the sixth grade at Challenger School."

I had some misgivings about sending Shoeless to the food bank to represent us, so I suggested that one of us should go with him. "It's always best to work in pairs," I said.

"I'll go," Abby said.

"Maybe they'll give us brownies," Shoeless said. "Or cans of Pepsi."

"We aren't accepting any food, even if they offer it," Abby said. "We're only going for information, to find out what Sophie's family needs to do in order to receive food from the food bank."

"You expect me to give up part of my Saturday if there's no food involved?" Shoeless said. "No way. I'm a growing boy. I need sustenance."

"I'll bring you a muffin," Abby said.

"Deal," said Shoeless as he wiggled his ears at her.

The talk of brownies and muffins made me hungry. Usually I bring two snacks to school, one for mid-morning and one for the afternoon. I keep candy bars, cookies, and small bags of chips in my dresser drawer, but that morning I had been so focused on getting the food for Sophie out of the house without Mom noticing it that I had forgotten to pack anything from my goodie drawer.

The clock hands seemed reluctant to pass two, but class finally ended and we were excused. The six of us rushed to the supply closet, grabbed our groceries, and hurried out to the front of the school to meet Chance. Lauren, Abby, Hunter, and Shoeless left their food with Jelly Bean and me, then headed for their respective buses.

I stood at the curb with Jelly Bean, hoping Chance wouldn't forget. "If your brother doesn't show up, we're in trouble," I said.

"He'll be here. I texted him as soon as school got out, to remind him."

"Are you sure he got your text? Did he answer?"

"He got it. That dude can't go five seconds without checking his phone."

Less than a minute later, Chance clattered to the curb in a clunker car. He unlocked the trunk, and we hefted all the groceries inside. I climbed in the backseat, while Jelly Bean rode shotgun. Duct tape crisscrossed the window next to me and a wad of stuffing stuck out of a rip in the upholstery.

Since Jelly Bean didn't introduce me, I said, "Hi, Chance. I'm Emmy."

"Yo," said Chance.

"Thanks for doing this."

"Yep." Or maybe he said, "Uh." It was hard to tell. Even though he answered me, Chance kept his eyes on his phone, obviously reading a text message.

"Here's the address and how to get there," I said, handing a piece of paper to Jelly Bean. "I printed directions from MapQuest last night."

Jelly Bean read Sophie's address out loud.

"It's near the gravel pit," I said.

The car belched exhaust fumes as we pulled away from the school. Jelly Bean told Chance when to turn, and Chance must have heard because he followed instructions, but he never spoke again. I felt as if a robot was driving the car. Chance kept glancing at his phone to read text messages. He held the phone in his right hand and, although he kept the back of that hand on the steering wheel, his right thumb skipped across the keyboard as he sent texts.

In my state, it's not legal to text while you're driving. It isn't legal to talk on a cell phone while driving, either, unless you're wearing a hands-free headset, but I didn't say anything. Chance was doing us a favor and if we continued to help Sophie, we would need to ask him to drive us again. I didn't think he would appreciate criticism from the backseat.

Ten minutes later, we turned onto East Sycamore, Sophie's street. Chance slowed while we watched for number 1135.

"There it is," I said. The stucco building showed only a faint memory of sand-colored paint. It had no carport or assigned parking spaces. We had to park half a block away.

"I'll wait with the car," Chance said. "This is the kind of neighborhood where, if you leave your car unguarded for five minutes, your hubcaps get swiped."

I doubted that anyone would want to steal hubcaps or any other parts from this particular car, but it was good to know that Chance could speak in complete sentences.

"I could wait with the car while you carry the groceries," Jelly Bean suggested.

Chance did not bother to answer. He gave Jelly Bean a look that made it clear who would be sitting behind the wheel and who would be carting the heavy bags of groceries.

Jelly Bean and I each took two bags out of the trunk and started toward Sophie's apartment building. The concrete walk leading to the front door buckled in the center where a tree root had snaked beneath it. The offending tree had been cut down, leaving a stump.

"Watch out," I warned, but Jelly Bean tripped on the uneven sidewalk anyway.

He lurched forward but managed not to fall, or to spill the groceries he carried.

The front door of the building was unlocked. We stepped inside and saw that apartments 1 and 2 were on the first floor, while apartments 3 and 4 were up a full flight of stairs.

"Apartment three," I said.

Jelly Bean groaned. "Up the stairs?"

"Up the stairs," I said, and we started climbing.

The air smelled like moldy bread, and the carpet on the stairs had worn so thin that the wood showed through.

We set the bags down in front of Sophie's door. Odd music that seemed to be mostly drums pulsed from inside apartment 4. I didn't hear any sounds coming from inside apartment 3, and I wondered if anyone was home.

It took Jelly Bean and me three trips, carrying as much as we could each time, to get all the groceries to Sophie's door. My legs ached from climbing the stairs with our heavy loads. After the last trip, I knocked on the door but we didn't wait to see if anyone came. We were halfway down the steps when we heard the door open.

A childish voice squealed, "Mama! Sophie! Look! Look!"

I couldn't see her, but I knew it had to be Trudy. I had goose bumps on my arms as I heard her joyful cries.

We tiptoed the rest of the way downstairs, and let ourselves out the door.

"That," said Jelly Bean, "was awesome."

"She sounded as excited as if we'd left her every toy she'd ever dreamed of."

"Toys don't matter much," Jelly Bean said, "when your stomach is empty." It wasn't the kind of comment I usually heard from Jelly Bean. For the first time, I wondered about his family. What was his home like? Was it possible that all of his talk about pizza and being hungry was for real? I had assumed he was only goofing around, pretending to be half starved. He had collected food for Sophie, and his brother had a car. If his family could afford a car for Chance, even a wreck like this one, they must have enough money for food.

Chance was so engrossed in his latest text message that he didn't notice when we got back to the clunkermobile. Jelly Bean rapped on the car window. Chance unlocked the doors, and we headed home, with me telling Chance how to find my house.

"This is a good project," Jelly Bean said. "I think we should do it again next week."

I agreed, and the next day the rest of our group did, too. Lauren got tears in her eyes when I told how excited Trudy had been to discover the bags of food. Everyone voted to collect food again, and Jelly Bean said he would ask Chance to drive us to Sophie's house on Tuesday.

Over the weekend, I put the food project out of my mind, except for Saturday afternoon when Mom said, "Emmy, have you seen those two tote bags that I bought at the Farmer's Market? I can't find them anywhere."

Oops. I should have used paper or plastic bags that Mom wouldn't miss. "I don't know where they are," I replied. That's true, I told myself. I knew where they were on Thursday afternoon when I left them outside Sophie's apartment, but I didn't know for sure where they were now.

On Monday when Mrs. Reed had us meet with our community service groups, Abby and Shoeless reported on their visit to the food bank.

"Sophie's family doesn't have to prove that they are low income, but they do have to prove that they live in Cedar Hill," Abby said. "When they show some ID with their address on it, they're given a food bank card."

"They don't even have to take ID the first time they go," Shoeless said. "If someone comes to the food bank and says they are hungry but don't have any ID, they're given a one-time voucher so that they can get food right away. Then they're asked to bring ID the next time."

"Sophie's mom might not have a driver's license," Lauren said. "That's what my mom uses for ID."

"All Sophie's mom needs is a recent piece of mail addressed to her that shows she lives in Cedar Hill," Abby said. "It could be the electric bill or the rent bill. Anything that reached her via U.S. Mail will work."

Riding the bus home on Monday, I told Lauren that I

probably wouldn't collect as much food as I had the first week. "I'm only going to the neighbors I know and I've already done nearly all the homes where someone is there after school. I can't go in the evening without my parents finding out."

"Why don't you come to my house and we'll collect food together?" Lauren asked. "There are lots of homes in my neighborhood where I haven't gone yet."

I quickly called Mom and told her I would be at Lauren's house for a couple of hours. "Be home before it gets dark," she said. "I'm going to be a little late tonight. I need to do some errands on my way home."

Lauren and I easily filled two bags each with donated food, including a bag of dry cat food.

"Jelly Bean lives on the next block," Lauren said. "Let's ask if we can put this in Chance's car now, instead of carrying it all to school tomorrow on the bus."

"Good idea."

Jelly Bean answered the phone. "I'll send Chance a text and ask him," he said, "but I don't see why not." He called back a few minutes later to say that would work.

Good, I thought. That removes any possibility of Mom seeing the food and asking about it. One less thing for me to worry about.

Chance wasn't there when we got to Jelly Bean's house, so he had us put the food in the garage. "I'll transfer it to the car tomorrow morning," he promised.

When I saw Jelly Bean's house, I quit worrying whether

he had enough to eat. His home looked much like mine—a well-kept rambler on a pleasant street.

As Lauren and I walked back to her house, I said, "Jelly Bean's been really helpful on this project."

Lauren agreed. "When Mrs. Reed gave us the assignment, I thought he and Shoeless would make it impossible to accomplish anything, but they've both been great."

The next morning when I opened my goodie drawer to get out my daily snacks, I paused. Nobody had donated treats for Sophie's family. Lauren and I had collected lots of nutritious food but not one person had given us dessert. Every kid likes something sweet now and then, I thought. I wondered how long it had been since Sophie and Trudy had eaten chocolate.

I got an empty plastic bag and put all the goodies from my drawer in it: two Hershey bars, a box of Gummy Bears, Fritos, some red licorice, and even an unopened bag of Reese's Peanut Butter Cups in red wrappers that I got at half price on the day after Valentine's Day. I had been saving these for a day when I really craved them.

I looked at the bulging bag of treats, hoping I would not regret giving them all away. I remembered the day I had forgotten to take snacks; I had done fine without them. I could skip them for a week or so.

I carried the bag of goodies to school in my backpack. At both the morning and afternoon recess, when I would usually have eaten a snack, I thought about Sophie and Trudy and how much they would enjoy eating my treats.

When Chance drove up to my school that afternoon, I added my bag of treats to the food we had collected.

The second food delivery was almost identical to the first, except this time after Jelly Bean and I knocked on the door and started down the stairs, we heard the door open and then a girl's voice called, "Thank you!"

It wasn't a little kid this time. This voice sounded about the same age as me. She didn't come to the top of the stairs and try to talk to us, but I knew it must be Sophie.

"You're welcome!" Jelly Bean called. He kept moving down the stairs, but I said, "I'll be down in a minute. I'm going to talk to her." I turned and ran back up the stairs.

A thin girl with thick dark hair had picked up a bag of groceries and started inside with it.

"Wait," I called.

She stopped, turned, and looked at me.

"Are you Sophie?" I asked.

She nodded.

"I'm . . ."

She interrupted, smiling at me. "I know who you are. You're my secret friend."

I laughed. "I'm Emmy," I told her.

"Thank you for bringing us food," she said.

"How old are you?" I asked.

"Ten." She paused, and then added, "I know. You're supposed to be eighteen to enter Dunbar's Dream Contest, but

I hoped whoever picks the winning entries wouldn't care. Or I thought maybe the judge would be a wealthy philanthropist who would choose to help us even if I didn't win the contest."

"Instead of a wealthy philanthropist, you got me," I said, "and my classmates."

"Hey," said Sophie. "I'll take you any time. The food you left last time was awesome. My family would be really hungry without you."

"There's a food bank in the Cedar Hill Community Center," I told her. "They're open every Tuesday, Thursday, and Saturday from ten until two. Your mom can get food for your family there. Tell her to take some identification with her."

Sophie frowned. "What kind of identification?"

"Anything that shows her name and that you live here. It can be a bill that's addressed to her at this address."

"When she's well enough to go there, I'll tell her," Sophie said, but something about the way she said it made me think it wouldn't happen. I wondered if it was hard for her to talk about her family's situation.

"What grade are you in?" I asked.

"Fifth. You?"

"Sixth. I go to Challenger School."

"How'd you get my contest entry?"

"My mom works at Dunbar's. She helps judge the contest."

"Did she get my thank-you letter?"

A cold, hard lump formed in the back of my throat. I swallowed. "I'm not sure," I said. I hope not, I thought. Mom and I had talked about Sophie's entry, so if Dunbar's got a thank-you note from Sophie, Mom would figure out that I had disobeyed her instructions about fulfilling a request, which meant I would be in a heap of trouble.

"I'm sorry I can't ask you to come in," Sophie said. "Mama's feeling worse and she's asleep. Trudy's taking a nap, too."

"I can't stay, anyway. My friend's brother drove me here, and he's waiting to drive me home."

As we talked, a small scrawny black cat padded toward us. He sat beside Sophie and began licking one paw and washing his whiskers.

"This is Midnight," Sophie said. "I found him eating a piece of a chicken leg that somebody had dropped near the Dumpster behind our building."

I leaned down to pet Midnight, who pushed his head against my hand and purred.

"I made a Found Cat sign," Sophie said, "but nobody claimed him, so he stayed with me." She scooped the little cat into her arms, and he snuggled against her, purring. "He is a very intelligent cat, and he thanks you for bringing him food and a toy."

"He's beautiful," I said.

"I was afraid Mama wouldn't let me keep him because we have to share our food with him, but when she saw how happy he makes me—and Trudy, too—she said he could stay."

"I'll try to bring more cat food next time," I said. "Do you need cat litter, too?"

"I use regular dirt, in an old dishpan. Midnight is a good boy and uses his pan."

She bent her head over the cat, who purred even louder.

"Why don't you write down your phone number for me?" I said. "I could call during spring break, to see if you need anything. I can give you my number, too. Just be sure to talk to me, not my mom."

"We don't have a phone. It got disconnected when we couldn't pay the bill."

"What about e-mail?" As soon as I asked, I realized what a dumb question it was. If you can't afford a phone, you don't have Internet access, either.

"No computer," Sophie said.

"I'll figure out a way to get in touch with you," I said.

"Thank you for helping us," Sophie said. "Mama was on the verge of moving to Mexico, even though we don't want to do that. Her parents are there—my grandparents."

It surprised me that Sophie had close family. Why didn't they help?

She must have read my mind. "My grandparents are poor themselves," she said, "and can't send us money, but they offer a home if we go to live with them." Her dark eyes looked fierce. "I am an American girl, and so is Trudy. We were born here, and we should stay here." Her voice dropped to a whisper. "But if Mama does not get well soon and find work again, we will have to leave."

"What about your dad?"

Sophie shook her head. "He's gone," she said. "He . . ."

"Hey, Emmy!" Jelly Bean bellowed from the bottom of the stairs. "Chance says we're leaving in sixty seconds."

"I have to go now, before Jelly Bean's brother leaves without me."

I wanted to hear more of Sophie's story. What did she mean by "gone"? Had her dad deserted the family? Was he dead?

Instead of asking my questions, I waved good-bye, dashed down the stairs, and climbed in the backseat of the clunkermobile.

"It took you long enough," Chance said.

"Sorry."

"I'm gonna be late for the basketball game."

"Sorry," I repeated.

The night before there had been a segment on the news about the rising cost of gasoline. It showed how much prices had gone up in the last few weeks, and it had occurred to me that Chance might appreciate it if he got some help filling the clunkermobile's gas tank.

Before I left home that morning, I had taken a five-dollar bill out of the shoe box where I keep the money I'm saving to buy a new bike. Now I fished in my jeans pocket for the money and handed it into the front seat. "This is for gas," I said. "For driving us."

Chance looked surprised, but he didn't say anything because his phone must have vibrated. He put the five dollars on the seat next to him and turned his attention to his latest text message.

All the way home, I thought what it would be like not to have a phone. No Internet. No e-mail or Facebook or texting my friends. No computer solitaire when I got bored. Even worse, Sophie had no dad. I missed my dad a lot when he worked out of town, but his absence was temporary. He called or e-mailed often, and I always knew he'd be home at the end of the week. Two weeks at the most. Dad wasn't ever gone the way Sophie had said the word, as if she knew her father would never be back.

I thought about what it would be like to live with the threat that I might have to move whether I wanted to or not—to leave my home, my friends, my school, or even my country. Most of all, I thought how it would feel to have no food except what strangers brought to the door.

CHAPTER FOUR

Mom got home about an hour after I did, bringing another batch of contest entries. While she changed into comfy clothes, I riffled quickly through the stack of entries.

If I saw an envelope that looked like Sophie's handwriting, I intended to remove it, but none of the envelopes were similar to the one that had come earlier. The thank-you letter must not have arrived yet, or maybe I had gotten lucky and Mrs. Murphy had opened it. She would assume that Help Your Neighbor had provided food for Sophie's family even though their funds are low.

I wandered into the kitchen and opened the fridge. To my surprise I had not missed my usual snacks, but I hadn't eaten since lunch and now I was starving. I was staring into the depths, hoping a chocolate mousse would miraculously appear on the shelf, when Mom came in.

"Don't stand with the door open," she said.

"I'm hungry. What's for dinner?"

"How about an explanation?"

"What?" I closed the fridge and turned to look at her.

"I understand you got a ride home from school today."

"How did you know that?"

"I saw Mrs. Braider outside when I picked up the mail."

That figures, I thought. Leave it to Big Mouth Braider to notice how I got home, and tattle on me.

"Who was your chauffeur?" Mom asked.

"Jelly Bean's brother, Chance, drove me home," I said. "Jelly Bean and I were working on our community service project after school and I missed the bus, so when his brother picked him up, they offered me a ride."

I thought it sounded like a great excuse and, even though it wasn't the whole story, everything I said was true.

Mom frowned. "You've been riding around with some teenager I know nothing about?"

"Chance has his driver's license," I said. "His parents knew he had the car and he had permission to take Jelly Bean home after school."

"That may be so, but you did not have permission to go anywhere with him. How do I know he's a good driver? Just because he has his license doesn't mean he's someone you should be riding with. I've never met this boy or his parents. Honestly, Emmy, I thought you had better sense."

"I'm here," I pointed out. "He brought me home safely, didn't he?"

"That's not the issue," Mom said. "You are not to accept a ride from someone I've never met."

"What if it had been Jelly Bean's mom? You've never met her, either. Would you be angry if she had driven me home?"

Mom rolled her eyes, as if I were being totally unreasonable.

"You're treating me like a baby," I said.

The phone rang, and I reached for it, glad for the interruption. I talked to Dad for a few minutes and then handed the phone to Mom. To my relief, she didn't tell him about Big Mouth Braider's report. While they talked, I decided to redeem myself by making a salad, warming up some leftover lasagna, and setting the table. By the time Mom got off the phone, dinner was ready.

We had finished eating when the phone rang again.

"Hello?"

"Emmy? Are you okay?" Lauren sounded breathless, as if she might be crying or had run a long way.

"I'm fine. Why wouldn't I be?"

"Oh, Emmy, it's horrible!"

"What? What's wrong?"

"I saw it on the TV news. Jelly Bean's brother hit a power pole and totaled his car!"

A chill ran down the back of my neck. "Is he okay? Was anyone with him?"

"That's the worst part!" Lauren wailed. "Jelly Bean was in the front seat."

I felt as if ice water flowed in my veins.

"They've both been taken to the hospital, and the reporter

said they have life-threatening injuries. Life threatening! That means—"

I interrupted. "I know what it means," I said.

"I thought you were in the car, too, because the accident happened about the time you would have been on the way home from Sophie's house."

I felt as if I'd been punched in the stomach. "It happened after they brought me home."

"Oh, Emmy," Lauren wailed. "What if Jelly Bean dies?"

I couldn't stand to think about that possibility. "I'm going to hang up and turn on the TV," I said. "What channel is it on?"

"Channel five."

As I clicked the remote, Mom asked me what was wrong.

I tried not to cry as I said, "Chance had a car accident. He and Jelly Bean were both hurt."

"Chance is the boy you were riding with?" Mom asked. "The one who brought you home?"

I nodded.

Mom's face turned pale, but she didn't say anything else. She didn't need to.

I had to wait through four commercials and the weather report before the news anchor said, "Now for an update on the breaking news we told you about at the top of the hour. A car went off the road in the twelve hundred block of East Cherry Street about four thirty this afternoon and slammed into a power pole." The screen filled with a picture of Chance's car. The clunkermobile's whole front end was smashed in, like a soda can that's been squashed for recycling.

Beside me, Mom gasped.

The report continued. "The driver, sixteen-year-old Chance Logan, was taken to Community Hospital. His younger brother, Jason, who was a passenger, was also hospitalized. Both are listed in critical condition. Police are investigating the cause of the accident, but no alcohol or drugs appear to have been involved."

I felt sick to my stomach. I had no doubt what had caused this horrific accident. Instead of paying attention to the road, Chance had been either reading a text message or sending one. I wondered what message had been so important that it was worth risking his life for. His life, and Jelly Bean's.

When the announcer went on to a different report, I clicked off the TV.

"I'm going to walk Waggy," I said. I needed to be alone, to think about what had happened.

I snapped the leash on Waggy's collar, trying to keep him from biting the leash in his excitement. Going for a walk is Waggy's second-favorite activity in the whole world. The first is getting food of any kind. Being petted by me, his loving person who begged and begged to rescue him from the animal shelter until my parents gave in and signed the adoption papers, comes in a distant third. After stuffing a plastic bag in my pocket and grabbing a flashlight, I slipped into my denim jacket and headed outside.

Tears blurred my vision as we walked, and a mixture of emotions churned through me—fear for Jelly Bean and his brother, plus the terrible knowledge that it could as easily have happened while I rode in the backseat, in which case I would probably be in the hospital, too.

It was bad enough for Mom to find out from Big Mouth Braider that I'd gotten a ride home with Chance. What would it have been like if she'd had a call from the police, telling her that I was in the hospital? Or dead?

Guilt pricked my conscience. I should have spoken up. I should have told Chance that it isn't legal or safe to text and drive. So what if he got angry at me for saying that? It might have made him stop. It might have prevented this awful crash.

While Waggy sniffed at trees, I thought of more reasons to feel guilty. If I had not gone back to talk to Sophie, Chance and Jelly Bean wouldn't have been on that particular street at that time. Chance wouldn't have been running late and hurrying to get to the basketball game. If I hadn't taken Sophie's contest entry to school, Chance and Jelly Bean would have gone home after school rather than delivering food to Sophie's family. At four thirty, Jelly Bean would have been safe in his own house, eating potato chips or an apple or a peanut butter sandwich instead of smashing into a power pole.

I knew it was irrational to blame myself, but I couldn't help feeling that if it had not been for me, this accident would never have happened.

When I got back with Waggy, Mom said, "I hope you see now why I want to know who you ride with."

"I'm sorry," I said.

She nodded and let it go. She thought I was apologizing for riding with someone she didn't know, but I was really sorry for a whole lot more than that. I just couldn't tell her about it.

At school the next morning, the student body buzzed with rumors about the accident. Hunter said the car had flipped over, pinning both boys inside. "The fire department had to use their Jaws of Life apparatus to get Jelly Bean out," Hunter said.

Crystal Warren rushed in, declaring that Jelly Bean had died. "My cousin's neighbor heard it on the radio," she said. "He died, and as soon as his brother wakes up, he's being arrested for vehicular manslaughter!"

None of us believed her, but it still made me uneasy to hear her say it.

As soon as class started, Mrs. Reed said, "I know you've all heard about Jason's accident and are wondering about his condition."

"He's dead!" Crystal blurted. "My cousin told me."

"Your cousin was misinformed," Mrs. Reed said. "Jason is alive, and he is expected to make a full recovery."

"Oh," said Crystal as the rest of us relaxed a little.

"I spoke with Jason's father about an hour ago," Mrs. Reed said. "Both boys will be hospitalized for a while. Jason has a broken leg, three broken ribs, and a concussion, but he is no longer in the Intensive Care Unit. His brother's injuries are more serious. Chance is still in a coma."

Nobody spoke.

"Do you have any questions?" Mrs. Reed asked.

Abby raised her hand. "Is a coma when the person's asleep and can't wake up?"

"He isn't asleep," Mrs. Reed explained. "He's unconscious.

Most people in comas gradually regain consciousness after a few days."

Most people, I thought, but not all of them do. I remembered a much publicized case of a woman who had been in a coma for several years and when her husband filed for a divorce, her parents had a fit. He claimed he still loved her, but he wanted to live a normal life and be free to date other women and possibly get married again. My parents had discussed the case while we ate dinner one night, agreeing that such a dilemma had no easy answer.

When there were no other questions, Mrs. Reed said, "I thought you might each like to make a card for Jason. I can deliver them to the hospital."

I felt relieved to have something specific to do for Jelly Bean. A card wouldn't heal his broken bones or take away the pain, but at least he would know his classmates were thinking about him, and that might make him feel a little bit better.

Mrs. Reed put out an assortment of colored paper, rubber stamps, crayons, glue, glitter, and other craft supplies, and we got busy.

"Don't use the purple crayon," warned Crystal. "Purple crayons cause chicken pox."

"All of the crayons are perfectly safe," said Mrs. Reed.

I made two cards, one for Jelly Bean and one for Chance. I almost wrote "I'm sorry" on Chance's card, but I settled for Get Well Soon. On Jelly Bean's, I drew a picture of a dog and printed HEAL! in large letters. I hoped Jelly Bean would think my pun was funny.

I could hear Shoeless and Hunter mimicking Crystal. "Don't use the yellow crayon," Shoeless whispered. "If you do, all your hair will fall out."

"Beware the gold glitter," Hunter replied. "Gold glitter causes toenail fungus."

"Never put blue paint on green paper," Shoeless said, "or you'll . . ." He whispered the rest in Hunter's ear and the two of them tee-heed while the rest of us wondered what horror would supposedly result from blue paint on green paper.

Hunter and Shoeless snickered and giggled until Mrs. Reed said, "That's enough, boys. No more jokes."

As I worked on my creations, I thought about our community service project. Without Chance to drive us, we had no way to get groceries to Sophie's family again. If Chance recovered, he probably wouldn't have a car to drive, and, even if he did, I couldn't ride with him anymore.

The rest of the kids in my community service group had apparently been thinking the same thing because when Mrs. Reed had us meet after lunch to finish our projects, Hunter said, "There's no point collecting more food if we don't have a way to deliver it."

Shoeless said, "I think we should write up a report of what we already did and turn it in and be done."

"And not help Sophie anymore?" Abby said.

"Our assignment was to do a community service project," Shoeless said, "and we did it. Nobody said we have to keep doing it forever."

Lauren turned to me. "Did you tell Sophie about the food bank?" she asked.

"Yes. I told her where it is and when it's open and that her mom should take some ID with her."

"Then they don't need us anymore," Hunter said.

"Her mom's too sick to go to the food bank," I said.

"That isn't our problem," Shoeless said.

"I feel sorry for her," Abby said, "but I agree with Shoeless. We've done as much as we can to help."

Hunter said, "When we decided to do this, I thought all we would do is go around our neighborhoods once and collect food. We'd help the kid who entered the contest, and we'd get credit for our community service project, and that would be the end of it. Well, we did that. In fact, we did it twice. We can't feed that family forever. They're apparently as needy now as they were when we got into this."

Abby said, "We didn't cause the problem. Why should we have to fix it?"

Lauren said, "Because we should always try to help others, if we can."

"There are places like the food bank," Hunter said, "to help people. There are other social service agencies, too, and sometimes community groups that can help."

"I don't want to collect food forever, either," I said, "but I think we should continue until Sophie's mother is well enough to go to the food bank."

"What's wrong with her mother?" Hunter asked.

I admitted that I didn't know.

"What if she has some really bad disease?" Hunter asked. "Maybe she isn't ever going to get well."

I stared down at my hands. I'd had the same fear, but I hadn't wanted to admit it.

"We helped Sophie," Hunter said. "It isn't as if we ignored the situation."

I wondered if my classmates would feel so negative about continuing if Chance had not driven his car into a power pole. Did the accident, and Jelly Bean being injured, seem to them to be the fault of our project, the same as it did to me? But none of them knew about Chance's texting while he drove. I was the only one who felt guilty for not trying to put a stop to that.

"All the community service projects need to wrap up this week," Abby pointed out, "so that the reports can be turned in by Monday. We have to officially end our involvement regardless of whether we want to keep taking food to Sophie or not."

"Good," said Shoeless. "Because I'm done with it."

"So am I," said Abby.

"I'm glad we did it," Hunter said, "but I'm relieved it's over, too."

Instead of planning another food delivery, my group wrote up our community service project report, and Abby took it home to make copies.

Lauren looked at me.

"We need to talk," I said.

CHAPTER FIVE

As Lauren and I walked to the bus after school, she said, "What should we do about Sophie?"

"I don't know. We can't quit taking food without being sure that Sophie and her family are okay. I know we aren't responsible for them, but since we know about their trouble, I feel as if I have to help."

Lauren nodded. "The question is, how? It'll be hard for only two of us to keep providing enough food, especially if we don't have a way to get it there."

"We need to talk to Sophie," I said, "and find out exactly what the situation is. She started to tell me about her father. Maybe he can be contacted and would help. Maybe there are other family members here in the United States."

Lauren said, "I also think Hunter is right; we should find out what's wrong with her mom."

"So we need to go to Sophie's house and talk to her," I said.

"How are we going to get there?"

"On the city bus, I guess."

"If we're going to go there, we might as well take some more food," Lauren said. "I have a piano lesson today, but I could collect food on Friday."

We agreed to collect food in another section of the housing development where Lauren lived, and to check the bus schedules to find out how to get to Sophie's house.

The next morning, Mrs. Reed said, "You will be happy to know that Jason is much improved and is allowed to have visitors as long as there are only two people at a time in his room."

Right away everyone started yammering about going to visit Jelly Bean. Shoeless suggested we each contribute money to buy Blizzards from Dairy Queen, and he would take them to the hospital. "Snickers Blizzards," he said, "or Milky Ways." This started a debate about which flavor Blizzard tastes best.

Mrs. Reed clapped her hands to quiet us down. "Jason's father suggested that the class select one person to represent all of you and that I take that one person for a brief visit tonight." She looked at Shoeless. "We will not be taking any food with us."

I thought for sure the class would select Shoeless to be the visitor, since he and Jelly Bean always hung out together at school, but instead they chose me.

"Emmy was the last person from our class to see him before the accident," Abby said, when she nominated me, "so I think Emmy should be the one to go to the hospital."

When I won by three votes, I could tell Shoeless was disappointed. Mrs. Reed seemed relieved.

"I'll call your parents," Mrs. Reed told me, "to make sure it's all right with them." She arranged to pick me up at 6:45.

I nibbled at my dinner, uneasy about going to see Jelly Bean. The only time I'd visited anyone in the hospital was when my grandma had her knee replaced. I had wanted to see her after the surgery, but when I got there, her pale face shocked me. My grandma is one of those cool old people who's interested in what goes on in the world and who pays attention when kids talk, but that day she had been given pain pills, so she was sleepy and barely said anything to me. The whole thing creeped me out. In a day or two Grandma was home and back to her usual chatty self, but the experience had left me wary of hospital visits.

"You don't have to go if you don't want to," Mom said. I swear the woman is psychic sometimes. I hadn't said one word about not wanting to go.

"I want to go," I said. I really didn't, but there was no way I could back out after my classmates had voted me to be the one to visit Jelly Bean.

"I thought you might want to take him a gift," Mom said as she handed me a new DVD. It was the movie I'd coveted for months, so I figured she had bought it as a present for me and had been saving it for my birthday.

"Thanks," I said. "He'll like this." I wondered if she'd buy another one for me or if I'd get one less gift in order to take a DVD to Jelly Bean. I was surprised to realize that I didn't care.

The DVD that I had wanted so badly didn't seem important now. I'd rather give it to Jelly Bean than keep it. Maybe it would help me to feel less guilty about the accident.

Mrs. Reed arrived promptly at 6:45 and told Mom she'd have me home by eight.

When we got to the hospital, she stopped at the reception desk. "Which room is Jason Logan in?" she asked.

Jelly Bean was on top of the covers with the head of the bed elevated, playing a computer game on a laptop. He wore blue striped pajamas and had a little plastic bracelet on his wrist. A cast encased the bottom half of his left leg, and that foot was propped up on two pillows. That pajama leg had been cut from ankle to knee, in order to accommodate the cast.

Jelly Bean's dad greeted Mrs. Reed, who introduced me. Then his dad said he and Jelly Bean's mom, who was in Chance's room, would be in the cafeteria for a while.

"Want to sign my cast?" Jelly Bean asked, handing me a box of markers. I chose a green one, and wrote my name. There were already several other names in various colors, including a bright red one that said SHOELESS.

"Shoeless was here?" I said.

"He came about an hour ago," Jelly Bean said. "He brought me a Snickers Blizzard from Dairy Queen."

"Why am I not surprised?" Mrs. Reed said.

"Do you want to sign my cast, too, Mrs. Reed?" he asked.

"Absolutely." She took a deep purple marker and not only signed her name but embellished it with curlicues. Jelly Bean grinned when he saw it.

"How's Chance?" I asked.

Jelly Bean quit smiling, and I was sorry I'd asked. "The same," he said.

I gave him the DVD, and then we chatted a while about school and the spring band concert that was scheduled for the following week. Jelly Bean plays trumpet in the school band but would have to miss the concert.

"The one good thing about this," Jelly Bean said, "is that I don't have to do any homework."

"What makes you think that?" Mrs. Reed said. "I'm saving it for you to do after spring break." Then she laughed at Jelly Bean's expression and said, "Only kidding."

When Jelly Bean's dad returned, Mrs. Reed and I said our good-byes. Mrs. Reed gave Jelly Bean the cards my class had made, and as we left he had already started reading them.

As we stepped off the elevator in the lobby, I spotted a familiar face. Why was Sophie here?

"Excuse me a minute," I told Mrs. Reed. "That girl is a friend of mine."

I hurried over to Sophie, who was as surprised to see me as I was to see her.

"Why are you here?" I asked.

"Mama's here." Sophie's eyes brimmed with tears. "She was admitted last night."

"What's wrong with her?"

"She has pneumonia."

Relief swept through me. Sophie's mom didn't have some horrible terminal illness. "My grandpa in Florida had pneumonia last year," I said, "and now he's back playing golf and building birdhouses in his workshop."

"Mama's very sick, because she waited so long to come."

"Who's taking care of Trudy?"

"One of Mama's friends from Burger Barn, where she used to work before she got sick, is babysitting tonight. I stayed home from school today."

"I'm with Mrs. Reed, my teacher," I told her. "You could meet her, and she might be able to help."

Sophie shook her head. "No!" she said. "No, don't tell anyone that Mama's here."

"Mrs. Reed is—"

"Please! I know you want to help, but there are things you don't know, and you would only make it worse for me."

"Okay," I said. "Lauren and I plan to bring food for your family again. Maybe I'll see you then."

Sophie put a hand on my arm. "You have been a good friend," she told me. "Thank you for helping us, and for helping Midnight. Thank you for everything."

Later, I wondered why she had used the past tense. Why didn't she say, "You are a good friend," instead of "You have been a good friend." It was almost as if she was saying good-bye, as if she knew we'd never see each other again.

I went to Lauren's house after school the next day. Before we started out to collect more food, we went online and looked up the bus route we would need to take to get from school to Sophie's house.

"There isn't a direct route," Lauren said. "We'll have to take one bus downtown, transfer, and take a different bus to Sophie's street."

I wrote down the bus numbers and the times. "It's going to take us nearly an hour each direction," I said, "but I don't know any other way to get the food there."

"We could call a taxi," suggested Lauren.

"I'm trying to save my money for a new bike," I said. "I don't have extra for cab fare."

"The bus won't be too bad," Lauren said. "Coming home, we won't have heavy bags to carry."

We collected food in her neighborhood again, easily filling two more bags each. When we got back to Lauren's house she said, "My cousin is coming for the weekend, so I can't go to Sophie's until Monday. We can store the food in my sister's closet. She's away at school."

"Monday works for me," I said. "Maybe Sophie's mother will be home by then."

As soon as I got home from Lauren's house, I took Waggy for a long walk. When we came back, Mom was cutting up fruit for salad while vegetable soup simmered on the stove. My stomach grumbled. Not only had I put my usual mid-afternoon treat in the bag for Sophie, I had also skipped an after-school snack because Lauren and I were busy collecting more food. No wonder I was hungry!

The simple meal tasted delicious. Since I had not eaten any junk food all day, I decided this could be a Low Fat Day.

I didn't even put butter on my bread.

Dad got home late Friday night. He was worn out from working long hours in Alaska, so all he wanted to do on Saturday was watch some baseball, eat Mom's cooking, and nap. I heard Mom bring him up to date on Chance's condition. I knew she had told him on the phone about the accident and how I was almost in the car. I tensed, waiting for Dad to lecture me, but he said only, "I'm sure Emmy learned a lesson from this."

I felt antsy all weekend, unable to settle down to anything. On Saturday morning I walked to the Farmer's Market and bought two tote bags to replace the ones I'd left at Sophie's house. I always enjoy strolling around the market, admiring the fresh fruit, vegetables, and baked goods, but that day I kept wondering how children in my town could be hungry when there was such an abundance of good food. Usually I eat a doughnut at the Farmer's Market; that day I was content to look.

When I got home, I hid the bags in the pantry. I knew Mom would think they had been there all along, and that she had forgotten where she'd left them.

I spent most of Saturday afternoon and evening in my room, reading, playing computer games, and surfing the Internet. At three I called Community Hospital and asked about Chance's condition. I was told that the hospital could confirm that Chance was a patient there, but they could not release any specific medical information.

I called again an hour later. That time I asked for the Intensive Care Unit, but when my call was transferred the ICU nurse told me the same thing.

Since Lauren lived in Jelly Bean's neighborhood, I called her to see if she had any news.

"Jelly Bean's uncle set up a CaringBridge page for him and Chance," she said. "It's a web site where families can post updates about someone who's sick or injured. Instead of having to answer dozens of e-mails and phone calls, they post any changes on their CaringBridge page. Friends and family can go there to get the latest news. You can leave comments, too."

"What a great idea," I said. "Will you send me the link?"

As soon as Lauren e-mailed me the link to the Logans' CaringBridge page, I clicked on it and signed in. Jelly Bean's mom had posted an update an hour earlier:

Chance has been awake since early this morning. He is not yet talking but his eyes are open, and he responds to commands to blink once for yes and twice for no. Although the doctors say it is too soon to predict whether or not he'll make a full recovery, we feel optimistic.

Relief sent a tingle down my arms. I rushed downstairs to tell Mom and Dad. If Chance recovered, I could quit beating myself up for not warning him against texting and driving.

On Monday morning, Mrs. Reed told the class that Jelly Bean would be going home from the hospital that day.

"When will he be back in school?" asked Hunter.

"Oh, he won't be in our class again," said Crystal. "Concussions cause brain damage and he probably has the mind of a five-year-old now."

"Are you sure?" asked Abby.

Crystal nodded. "If he comes back at all, he'll most likely be in kindergarten."

"Where in the world did you hear that?" Mrs. Reed said.

Crystal frowned. "I read case histories of concussions on the Internet," she said.

"Don't believe everything you read online," Mrs. Reed said. "Anybody can post anything on the Internet, whether it's true or not."

"His brain seemed fine Thursday night, when I saw him in the hospital," I said.

"I visited him yesterday afternoon," said Shoeless. "We played gin rummy and read the latest *Sports Illustrated* together." He wiggled his ears up and down.

"There is not a thing wrong with Jelly Bean's brain," said Mrs. Reed.

"He must eat a lot of radishes," said Crystal.

We all gaped at her, but nobody asked what radishes had to do with the state of Jelly Bean's brain.

We didn't want to know Crystal's opinion.

CHAPTER SIX

I left for school half an hour early on Monday morning and walked to Lauren's house in order to help carry the bags of groceries to the school bus.

When school got out, Lauren and I removed the groceries from the supply closet, where Mrs. Reed had let us put them, and started down the street to the city bus stop. We waited nearly fifteen minutes before the number six bus rolled up and we climbed on board. We didn't talk much. I watched out the window, to be sure we got off at the right stop. I think Lauren was worried about that, too. We followed our progress on the map we'd printed off the transit company's website, and we disembarked at the right place.

Ten minutes later, we boarded the number fourteen bus, headed for Sophie's neighborhood.

By the time we walked up the uneven sidewalk to Sophie's door, we were both tired. We climbed the stairs to apartment 3 and knocked on the door. Nobody answered.

"Sophie?" I called. "It's Emmy."

Silence.

We knocked again.

The door to apartment 4 opened and a scruffy young man with three earrings in each ear said, "Nobody's home there. I think they moved."

"Moved!" I said. "Are you sure?"

"Nobody's been here since last week when the ambulance came. The mom got carried out on a stretcher, and the kids trailed along after it."

"They haven't moved out," I said. "They're only staying somewhere else while the mom is hospitalized."

He shrugged. "Whatever."

"Meow." The scrawny black cat crept out from behind an old broom that leaned against the wall in the corner of the hall. "Meow."

"Midnight!" I said. "What are you doing out here?"

"Meow!"

I squatted down, holding my hand out toward Midnight. He hesitated, then approached and sniffed my fingers.

"Dang cat's driving me nuts," the man said. "It cries and scratches on their door all night long."

"Have you fed him?" I asked.

"It ain't my cat," the man said. "Why would I feed him?"

"The poor thing is hungry," I said.

I dug in one of the grocery bags, lifted out a bag of dry cat food, ripped off a corner of the bag, and shook some food onto the floor. Midnight began eating.

"We brought some food for the little girls who live here," I said. "We'll leave it here, and if they don't come back in a few days, you can have it."

"Okay," he said. "Leave as much as you want."

I held out the bag of cat food. "Would you feed Midnight and give him a bowl of water?"

"Not me," he said. "I don't like cats, especially black ones. Black cats bring bad luck."

"That isn't true," Lauren said. "That's a silly superstition."

"Whatever."

Lauren and I glanced at each other. I wanted to give this guy a lecture about kindness and common sense. Either that or a good hard kick in the shin.

Instead, I asked him, "By any chance, do you have a Post-it note that I could have?"

"A what?"

I held up my fingers to indicate the size and said, "Those little papers that have stickum on the back."

He shook his head. I don't think he knew what I meant.

I ripped a three-inch square piece off the top of one of the paper grocery bags, then rooted in my backpack for a pencil. *Dear Sophie: Call me!* I put down my phone number, and signed the note *Emmy (Your Secret Friend).*

"I don't suppose you can give us a piece of tape," Lauren said to the man.

"Nope. No tape," he said.

I wedged the note into the crack of Sophie's door as hard as I could, hoping she'd find it. I did not believe she had moved because she would never move and leave Midnight behind. Probably her mother remained in the hospital, and Sophie was staying elsewhere and had no way to get home to take care of her cat.

The man abruptly closed the door to apartment 4, leaving Lauren and me—and Midnight—in the hall.

"Thanks for nothing," I muttered.

"I think his name is No Help," Lauren said.

"If we leave the bags of food here," I said, "No Help will grab them the second we're out the front door."

"You're probably right," Lauren agreed, "but I don't want to carry them home on the bus."

"Neither do I."

Lauren and I left all the groceries except the cat food in front of apartment 3. As we walked down the stairs, Midnight followed.

"Midnight would be better off outside," I said. "He can drink from the puddles." I opened the door and let Midnight go out.

I headed around the side of the building. "I'll leave the open bag of cat food behind the Dumpster," I said. "He was hanging around the Dumpster when Sophie found him, so he'll probably go there to scrounge for food."

"He's following us," Lauren said.

Midnight rubbed against my legs as I tore a larger hole in

the side of the cat food bag and put it in back of the Dumpster. I was afraid if I set it in front where it was easily seen, someone would pick it up and throw it away.

As soon as I put the bag down, Midnight started crunching on the food.

"That bag should last him until Sophie's family comes back," I said.

As Lauren and I walked to the bus stop, she said, "We need to find out what's going on with Sophie. I'm pretty sure she'll never see one ounce of the food we just left, even if she comes home today."

I agreed. "My grandpa says people who are kind to animals can be trusted," I said, "but be wary of those who aren't."

"I think your grandpa's right," Sophie said. "No Help wouldn't even feed a hungry cat when he knew the cat's family was away."

"I wish I'd asked Sophie what her last name is," I said. "If we knew that, we could call the hospital and find out her mom's room number, and go there."

"Maybe we can find her address online, and see who lives there," Lauren suggested. "Then we'd have the last name."

"Good idea."

"I'll do that tonight," she said, "and let you know if I learn anything."

We boarded the bus and found seats together. I felt lucky to have a friend like Lauren, who felt the same way I did about important things such as helping Sophie and feeding a hungry cat.

By the time we had transferred to the second bus, I was already worrying about Midnight. "Midnight was used to being indoors," I said. "I'm surprised that Sophie left him out in the hall. I would have thought she'd leave him shut inside with lots of food and water and his pan of dirt."

"Maybe he escaped when she wasn't watching," Lauren said. "My cat did that once, and we didn't even know he was gone until one of our neighbors called to tell us that Gus was on top of their car sleeping in the sun."

I envisioned Sophie calling 911 because her mother was so sick. An ambulance came, and Midnight got scared with all the commotion. While the emergency medical workers rolled a gurney out the door, he bolted. I wondered if No Help had let Sophie use his phone to call the medics. Probably not.

All I wanted to do when I got home was veg out in my room, but Mom had volunteered to bake cookies to serve after the school's band concert, and she wanted me to help. Usually, I'd be happy to roll out cookie dough, cut it into fancy shapes, and snitch as much raw dough as I could when Mom wasn't looking. That night, I was too worried about Sophie and her mom and Midnight to get into the spirit of baking cookies.

Also, now that I skipped the treats at recess and after school, I found I didn't miss them. As my craving for sugary snacks diminished, healthier food tasted better. I didn't intend to diet, but I wasn't going to gobble goodies any more, either.

Mom noticed that I didn't eat any of the warm cookies.

"Do you feel okay, Emmy?"

"I'm tired."

She reached over and put her hand on my forehead. "You don't seem to have a fever. We can wait until tomorrow to frost these."

As soon as the last pan of cookies came out of the oven, I got ready for bed. Mom was narrowing down the contest entries to her top ten when I said good night. I realized that Sophie's thank-you letter had never come. One more worry to stir into my pot of problems.

Although I was tired, it took me a long time to fall asleep. I kept wondering what had happened in Sophie's family that made her refuse to meet Mrs. Reed and reluctant to go to the food bank. When Waggy curled up beside me, I wondered where Midnight was spending the night.

Rain tap-danced on the roof over my bed. I hoped Midnight had found a place to stay dry. He was such a small cat, in such a harsh neighborhood.

As soon as I got on the school bus the next morning, Lauren said, "I looked at the county real estate records and found out who owns the building where Sophie lives. It's a business called Winkowski Associates. The president is John Winkowski. I called his office. He wasn't available, so I told his secretary that I needed to contact my friend from school who lives in apartment 3 of the building on East Sycamore."

"Good thinking." While I'd been home fretting uselessly, she had taken action to try to solve our problem.

"I said I couldn't remember Sophie's last name and asked if

she could tell me what it is, but she refused. She said Winkowski Associates does not disclose any personal information about their tenants."

"No surprise."

"I told her Sophie's mom was in the hospital and I was trying to help them," Lauren continued, "but I don't think I should have said that."

"Why not?"

"Because she jumped on that news and started asking me a bunch of questions. Which hospital? What was wrong with her? Was anyone still staying in the apartment?"

"Uh-oh," I said. "I'll bet someone went right over there. Maybe Sophie's mom owes back rent."

"That's what I think, too," Lauren said. "Instead of Sophie finding our note, someone from Winkowski Associates probably found it and threw it away."

"We need to go back there," I said. "If the note is gone, we'll leave another note."

"Take tape this time," Lauren said.

"Can you go today?" I asked.

Lauren shook her head. "I have an orthodontist appointment after school. Let's go tomorrow."

We agreed to return the next day, but the more I thought about the situation, the more uneasy I felt. By the time school let out, I had decided to return to Sophie's apartment by myself. I left a voice-mail message for Mom, telling her I was finishing up my community service project and would be home in time for dinner. Then I caught the city bus on the first leg of the ride to Sophie's apartment.

The bags of groceries were gone. So was the note I'd wedged in the door. If Sophie had found it, I knew she would have found a way to call me by now.

No sound came from either apartment 3 or apartment 4. I knocked on Sophie's door and wasn't surprised when nobody answered. I'd brought a note with me, identical to the one I'd written the day before, and a roll of Scotch tape. I took them out of my jacket pocket and taped the note securely to the door.

Then I went downstairs and walked behind the building to see if the cat food had been eaten, but I never made it around to the back of the Dumpster because as I approached, I heard a soft meowing sound.

"Midnight?" I said. "Is that you?"

The meow came again, louder this time. I looked around, trying to figure out where he was.

"Midnight," I said. "Here, kitty, kitty, kitty."

The meow escalated into a mournful yowl.

I froze. The yowl came from inside the Dumpster!

CHAPTER SEVEN

The sides of the Dumpster were too high for me to see in. I needed something to stand on, and I needed a way to lift the cat out.

"I'll be right back," I told Midnight. I raced back inside, up the apartment stairs, and pounded on the door of apartment 4. No one responded. No Help had probably thrown Midnight in the Dumpster, like a piece of garbage. He had admitted he didn't like cats, and he'd made it clear that he didn't care if Midnight starved to death.

I clattered down the stairs and knocked on the door of apartment 2. I heard nothing. My fury boiled over like an erupting volcano. I banged my fist on Apartment 1. Wham! Wham! Wham! My hand stung, but I didn't care.

"Hold your horses," said a voice from inside. "I'm coming as fast as I can."

An elderly woman wearing a flowered pink dress and a blue cardigan sweater opened the door. Both her hands rested on a metal walker. A cloud of white hair frizzed around her wrinkled face, and wire-rimmed glasses perched on her nose.

"I'm sorry to bother you," I said. "I'm a friend of Sophie's, from apartment three. She isn't here because her mother's in the hospital, and somebody threw her cat in the Dumpster behind the building. Do you have a chair I can borrow?"

"Slow down," the woman said. "I don't hear as well as I used to. Now, what's this about a cat?"

"Sophie's pet cat, Midnight, is in the Dumpster," I said, speaking slowly and enunciating carefully. "I can hear him meowing, and I need to get him out, but I can't reach him. I need a ladder, or even a chair to stand on. Oh, and a container of some sort to lift him out, and maybe some rope."

"Who are you?" the woman asked.

"I'm Emmy. I'm Sophie's friend."

"I'm Mrs. Spangler. Rose Spangler."

"How do you do?" I said. "Do you have something I can use to get me high enough to see inside the Dumpster?"

Mrs. Spangler backed up, pulling the walker after her, then turned around and headed toward her kitchen. I followed. "Would that work?" she asked, pointing to a step stool, the kind that folds flat but has two steps when it's opened.

"That's perfect!" I said. "Is it okay if I borrow it?"

"You're not going to jump down inside the Dumpster, are you?" Mrs. Spangler asked. "It isn't sanitary in there."

I wrinkled my nose and shook my head.

"Good, because you might not get back out."

"That's why I need something that I can lower down for Midnight to sit in while I pull him out. An empty box, maybe, or a basket." I looked around Mrs. Spangler's tidy apartment. Lace doilies covered the arms of an overstuffed chair, and framed photos flanked a small TV set.

"My laundry basket might work," Mrs. Spangler said. "It's in the bedroom."

She led the way and I followed, wishing she could move more quickly. She opened her closet door and showed me a wicker laundry basket with a few clothes inside. "Dump the dirty clothes on the floor," she instructed, "and take the basket."

"Thank you!" I said. "Now all I need is rope or twine. I can tie it on the basket's handle, and lower the basket down, and then, when Midnight gets in it, I'll pull him out."

"I don't have rope," Mrs. Spangler said, "but I have yarn. I used to knit, before the arthritis bent my fingers too much. I still have a bag of yarn." She showed me the yarn, and I selected a thick skein the color of cotton candy. By using several strands, it would be sturdy enough to hold the weight of the basket with Midnight in it.

While I cut six lengths of the pink yarn and threaded them through the opening in the basket's handle, Mrs. Spangler returned to the kitchen. I heard the sounds of a cupboard door closing, and then an electric can opener. As I tied off the yarn, she called, "I have bait, so kitty will get in the basket."

She held out an open can of tuna.

"That's a great idea!" I said. "Thank you so much, Mrs. Spangler. You've been a huge help. I'll bring your things back as soon as I rescue Midnight."

I took the step stool out first and opened it next to the Dumpster. When I climbed up, I could see Midnight standing forlornly on a pile of trash. Eggshells, coffee grounds, wadded-up paper napkins, orange rinds, and plastic bags filled with unidentifiable items were mixed together in a horrible hodgepodge of odor.

Next I carried out the laundry basket and the can of tuna. I placed the tuna in the basket, climbed back up the step stool, and tried not to inhale as I lowered the basket over the side. Midnight smelled the tuna right away and stepped toward it.

Get in the basket, I thought as he sniffed and craned his neck forward, trying to reach the tuna without stepping into the wicker container. Luckily, he couldn't reach the tuna without getting into the basket. The second he stepped into the basket, I pulled on the yarn. Midnight turned when the basket moved, and for a second, I thought he was going to jump back onto the piles of garbage.

"Hey, kitty, kitty," I said. "Hi, Midnight. You're a good boy. Stay where you are now. Good kitty. Good Midnight."

My voice seemed to soothe him and, although his tail swished nervously, he stayed in the basket while I slowly hauled it up and over the top. As I lowered it to the top of the step stool, he leaped to the ground and ran.

I climbed down and put the can of tuna on the ground. "Here, Midnight," I called. "Here, kitty, kitty."

I thought he might be more likely to come if I moved away from the tuna, so I folded up the stool and returned it and the basket to Mrs. Spangler, who waited for me with her door open, peering anxiously out.

"I got him," I said. "The tuna did the trick."

"Where is he?" she asked.

"He ran off, but I'm sure he'll be back to finish his tuna. I left the can where he can find it."

She nodded.

"Would you like to keep him until Sophie comes home?" I asked. If Midnight was shut in Mrs. Spangler's apartment, he would be safe until Sophie came looking for him.

"I wish I could," she said. "I always had animals in the old days—dogs and cats and once even a pet rabbit named Ralph. Ralph chewed through all my electric cords, but I loved him, anyway. I can't take care of an animal anymore, though. It's all I can do to keep myself going. I can't lift an animal or bend enough to clean up a mess."

"Thank you so much for helping me," I said as I put the step stool in her kitchen.

"What if whoever threw him in there does it again?" she asked.

That awful possibility had occurred to me, too. If No Help had dumped Midnight once because the cat cried outside Sophie's door or attempted to get into the apartment building whenever the front door opened, he might try to get rid of Midnight a second time. I didn't want him to have another chance.

"I'm going to take the kitty home with me," I said.

Until the words came out of my mouth, I had not considered taking Midnight with me, but once I said that, I knew it was the only way to be sure No Help didn't harm him.

"My parents will let me keep him until I can give him back to Sophie," I said.

I was not at all sure my parents would let me keep Midnight but I spoke confidently, as if by convincing Mrs. Spangler, I was also convincing Mom and Dad.

I untied the yarn, and wiped off the basket with a soapy cloth before I returned it to Mrs. Spangler's closet. I tossed the clothes from the floor into it.

Mrs. Spangler smiled, her blue eyes twinkling. "This is the most excitement I've had in a year," she said. "I don't get many visitors and now I've had two in one week. First the girl upstairs needed to make a phone call, and now you needed help to rescue a cat. For once I'll have something interesting to tell my daughter the next time she calls."

I promised myself that I'd return sometime to visit her, but right then I wanted to get back out to the Dumpster to catch Midnight. I hoped that getting thrown in the Dumpster had not made him so scared of people that he wouldn't come to me.

Mrs. Spangler waved as I left. "Come back any time," she said. "Let me know how kitty gets along in his new home."

As I rounded the back corner of the building, I saw Midnight sitting beside the empty tuna can, washing his whiskers.

"Hey, kitty, kitty," I said. "Hey, Midnight."

He strolled over and rubbed his head against my ankles. I let my breath out in relief. Then I scooped him up, held him against my chest, and headed for the bus stop.

A boy who appeared to be a year or two older than I am waited for the bus.

"Animals aren't allowed on the bus," he said as I stopped beside him. "Once when my uncle and I were on the bus, some kid tried to bring his dog on board and the driver said he couldn't unless it was a service dog, like a Seeing Eye dog or a seizure alert dog."

"This is my seeing eye cat," I said.

"Yeah, right."

"The bus driver won't know," I said. "I'll put Midnight under my shirt."

The boy looked doubtful. "I wonder how much the fine is for hiding a cat on board," he said.

I shrugged. I hoped he didn't plan to give me away.

When I saw the bus approaching, I stuffed Midnight under my T-shirt and pulled my jean jacket shut, holding the cat against me with my left hand while my right hand dropped the fare into the slot.

Until then, Midnight had been fine with me holding him. He had snuggled against me and purred while we waited for the bus. Once he was under my shirt, however, he went berserk, struggling to get out. I hurried down the aisle, hunched over so that nobody would notice my abdomen popping up and down like a jumping bean. "Ouch!" I said as Midnight's sharp little toenails dug into my skin.

The boy I'd been talking to laughed. "Shh," he said, holding one finger to his lips.

"Oh!" I gritted my teeth as I slid into the seat by the window. As soon as I sat down, I lifted my shirt far enough to grasp Midnight's paws and make him quit raking my stomach.

Although there were plenty of empty seats, the boy plopped down beside me and watched me wrestle with Midnight.

"He's shredding me," I whispered.

"Move him so he's between your shirt and your jacket," the boy said.

I did as he suggested and it helped a little, but Midnight still squirmed so much that his toenails penetrated the T-shirt. "I wish I had my backpack to put him in," I said. "I'm going to bleed to death before I get this cat home."

"Put disinfectant on your stomach as soon as you can," the boy said. "It's easy to get an infection from a cat scratch."

"Oh, great," I said.

"Cat bites are even worse than cat scratches," he said, "so don't let him bite you."

I nodded grimly, imagining headlines worthy of Crystal: *Girl Dies While Rescuing Dumpster Cat*. Or maybe, *Doctor Sews Up Two Thousand Bloody Cuts on Sixth-Grader's Stomach*.

"I hope he doesn't have rabies," the boy said.

Rabies! Knowing the financial status of Sophie's family, I was sure Midnight had not been vaccinated. I began to have second thoughts about saving Sophie's cat.

It's too late now, I thought. Operation Cat Rescue has

started and I can't quit partway through. What could I do—turn Midnight loose on the bus?

"The treatment for rabies is painful," the boy said. "You have to get shots in your stomach."

I could have done without that bit of information. Was this kid deliberately trying to scare me or was he one of those people who speak without thinking what impact his words might have?

I thought we'd never get to my stop. When I pulled the cord, the boy stood up to let me out of my seat. "Good luck," he said.

The bus driver watched suspiciously in his mirror as I stood hunched over and clutching my jacket while I waited for the back door to open. I stepped down, and immediately pulled Midnight out from under my clothes.

"You're killing me," I told him. "You have to calm down."

He sniffed the air, looking innocent, and quit struggling.

It helped to have a fifteen-minute wait between buses. As soon as Midnight came out from under my clothes, he settled right down. I stuck one hand under my shirt and gingerly touched my skin. Then I looked at my fingertips, expecting them to be dripping with blood, but I saw only a trace of red.

The second I stuck Midnight under my jacket to board the second bus, he turned into Monster Cat again.

"What do you have up your shirt?" the bus driver asked as I dropped my coins in the coin catcher. He leaned toward me, squinting. If I said I didn't have anything, he'd know I was lying and might not let me board the bus, so I decided to throw myself on his mercy.

"It's a cat," I said. "Somebody threw him in a Dumpster and I rescued him and I don't have any other way to get him home."

"In a Dumpster, you say?"

"That's right. I heard him meow and when I climbed up to look, I saw him standing in the garbage."

"We don't allow animals on the bus," the driver said, "unless they're service animals."

"It's too far for me to walk home," I said. "I couldn't leave him where I found him or the person who threw him in the Dumpster would do it again."

The driver looked at me for a second, mulling it over. He glanced back toward the other passengers. There were only three people and none paid any attention to us.

"He could be my service cat," I said.

"I reckon that cat of yours is doing a big service," the driver said, "teaching you to be a kind person. Just don't let anyone else see him."

"Thanks," I said.

Midnight's squirming continued until I got off at my own street. By then my midriff felt as if I'd rubbed a cheese grater against it.

I tried to come up with a good explanation for Mom of where I got Midnight and why I needed to keep him. I already had Waggy so I couldn't use the argument that every kid should have a pet. One look at my scratched hands, not to mention my abdomen, would make *He followed me home* unbelievable.

I toyed with telling the truth, since it had worked so well with the bus driver. "My friend's mom is in the hospital and I don't know where my friend is staying, and there's nobody at home to take care of her cat." That sounded good until I began thinking what Mom would ask me. Then I knew that not knowing Sophie's last name would be a sure deal breaker. Plus Mom would want to know how we became friends if Sophie doesn't go to my school. The whole telling the truth bit would not work.

In the end, what I told Mom was true, but I also left out certain aspects of the story. I simply said, "I was going past a Dumpster and I heard meowing from inside. A nice old lady let me use a step stool, and I saw this cat in the Dumpster with all the garbage."

Mom looked pained. "Someone threw a live cat in a Dumpster?"

I nodded. "I got him out, which wasn't easy, and I was afraid if I let him go, whoever put him in there would do the same thing again, so I brought him home. I got a few scratches; I'm going to go put disinfectant on my hands." *And*, I thought but didn't say, *on my stomach*.

"We are not keeping him," Mom said. "Waggy is enough trouble without having him chase a cat through the house."

"I think I know who owns him," I said.

"If you know who owns him, why didn't you take him there?"

"It might take a few days to contact her."

Mom gave me her "you aren't telling me the whole story" look, so I headed to the bathroom before she could ask more questions. When I sprayed disinfectant on those scratches, I wanted to shriek at the top of my lungs. Instead, I bit down hard on a towel and hopped around the bathroom with the towel in my mouth until the sting subsided.

When I returned to the kitchen smelling like disinfectant, Waggy was lying on the small braided rug on the kitchen floor with Midnight snuggled beside him, purring and kneading his front toes in and out of Waggy's thick fur.

"Good dog," I said. Waggy's tail thumped the floor. "Look, Mom, Waggy likes having Midnight for a friend."

"Midnight? You know this cat's name?"

"We have to call him something, and Midnight seems like a good name for a black cat."

Mom said, "We have no supplies for a cat. He needs cat food and litter and a pan to put the litter in, and a scoop."

"I'll use my own money," I said. "Any chance that you'll drive me to the store?"

Mom sighed. "This is not a permanent arrangement," she said as she took her car keys off the table.

I had planned to shut Midnight in the bathroom while we were gone but he and Waggy seemed so happy together that I left them as they were.

I realized as I rode to the store that I should have taped a note for Sophie on her door, telling her that I have Midnight. She would be frantic if she came home and couldn't find him. She might knock on her neighbor's door and ask No Help if he'd seen Midnight. I was sure that he had put Midnight in the Dumpster. Would he tell Sophie what he'd done? If he did, and the Dumpster had been taken away by the trash collection company, Sophie would be grieving for a dead cat who was actually alive and cuddling with Waggy.

Mom had been reading contest entries when I got home. Sophie's thank-you letter should have arrived by now so I figured I was lucky and Mom wasn't the one who read it. Still, mail sent to a large company but not addressed to a particular person might take a while to reach the right department. Sophie's thank-you note could still show up and get me in trouble.

Well, I couldn't do anything about Sophie's letter. I had my hands full dealing with Sophie's cat. Cat supplies were more costly than I had anticipated. I bought a bag of dry food, four cans of moist food, a bag of litter, and a scoop. I still needed a pan to put the litter in but I was out of money. "A cardboard box will do," Mom said. "The cat is only going to need it for a day or two."

I hoped she was right.

CHAPTER EIGHT

On the way home from the store, Mom said, "I wonder who the cat belongs to. He's clearly been socialized."

"I think he belongs to a girl named Sophie. I saw her cat once and this one looks like him, and she lives near the Dumpster where I found him."

"As soon as we get home, you need to call this Sophie and ask if her cat is missing. We should have done that right away. Maybe you would not have needed to buy all this."

"I don't know her number," I said, "or her last name. I'll ask at school tomorrow."

Bus rides must work up a cat's appetite because Midnight dug right in when I fed him, even though he'd eaten a whole can of tuna when he came out of the Dumpster.

I, on the other hand, didn't have much of an appetite. My

stomach was sore from the cat scratches, and I had so many worries that I barely tasted my dinner.

After we finished eating, I took Waggy out for a walk. Normally I walk him right after school, but lately I had not been coming straight home so poor Waggy hadn't received as much attention as usual.

When we returned, Midnight climbed on my lap while I tried to watch a movie. *Beauty and the Beast* is one of my favorites, but that night I couldn't concentrate. I turned it off partway through, walked Waggy one last time, and went to bed early.

I was too tired to fix a bedtime snack. I should have fallen asleep instantly. Instead, I lay staring at nothing while Waggy twitched beside me, having one of his dreams where, I think, he's chasing a squirrel. His paws scrabble at the blanket and he makes soft yippy noises. He never seems to catch the squirrel in his dreams, just like in real life. He only quits when I nudge him and say his name.

I lay in bed and tried to figure out what secret Sophie's family had. Were they immigrants who came to this country illegally? Sophie said she and Trudy were born here, but maybe her parents had been smuggled into the United States from Mexico or some other country, and now her mother feared they would be deported.

My mind raced on. Maybe Sophie's mom was in the government's Witness Security Program. Perhaps she had identified a criminal and now the criminal's thugs were trying to find her, to get revenge. Maybe Sophie's dad was a murderer! But if Sophie's mom was in the Witness Security

Program, she'd have enough food and all the help she needed from the U.S. government. Her kids wouldn't be hungry.

What else could the secret be? I tossed and turned so much that Waggy jumped off my bed and slept on the rug.

Sophie's mother might be in trouble with the law. What if there was a warrant out for her arrest and that's why she had not wanted to check into a hospital? Maybe she was wanted for murder!

I knew it was pointless to keep thinking up possible reasons why Sophie was secretive. I needed facts, not speculation.

On the bus the next morning, I told Lauren what had happened to Midnight.

"So, where's the cat now?" she asked.

"He's at my house, and my mom is not happy about it. She hopes when I come home today, I'll know Sophie's last name and where she lives."

"You already know where she lives."

"If I admit that, I'll have to explain why I was there." We rode in silence for a few minutes. I thought how complicated my life had become because I had not been truthful. I hadn't lied to Mom, exactly, but every time I withheld some facts, the situation got worse.

"Let's go to the hospital," Lauren said. "If Sophie's mom is still there, Sophie might be there visiting her. We can talk to her and tell her you have Midnight and find out what she wants you to do."

It seemed like a long shot, but I didn't have a better idea.

As soon as school got out Lauren and I took a bus downtown, headed for Community Hospital.

"I hope nobody asks who we're visiting," Lauren said. "We should have brought some flowers or candy, as if we were taking a present to a patient."

When we entered the hospital lobby, we saw a small gift shop. Lauren bought a balloon that said GET WELL SOON on it. "I can give it to my neighbor when I get home," she said. "He sprained his ankle and is off work for a few days."

I bought a single red rose. I planned to give it to Sophie and let her give it to her mom.

"Let's split up," I suggested. "You take the odd-numbered floors and I'll take the even ones. We'll walk past all the rooms and look for Sophie. If you see a thin girl about ten years old with dark hair, come and get me."

"Don't forget the family waiting rooms that they usually have either by the elevators or next to the nurses' stations."

"How do you know that?"

"My uncle was hospitalized for two weeks, and we visited him a lot."

When we reached the elevator, we agreed to meet back there in half an hour. Then I got on, pushed "2" and the search began. I acted as if I knew where I was going so that nobody would stop me. I walked slowly past the open doors, glancing in each one. I felt embarrassed, as if I were snooping into other people's personal business.

In one room, several people stood around a bed, holding hands and singing "Amazing Grace." My skin prickled. Their loved one is probably dying, I thought. I wanted to pull the door closed to give them privacy, but I kept walking.

Two doors down, a TV blared a football game. Three young men clustered around the bed. An open box of pizza occupied the patient's small bedside table.

Across the hall, a man wearing a badge that said VOLUNTEER stood with a golden retriever next to the bed of a little boy, about six years old. The boy was bald, and a bag filled with some kind of liquid hung over the boy's shoulder while the liquid dripped through a tube into one thin arm. His face glowed as he petted the dog with his other hand.

The dog wore a green coat that said THERAPY DOG. She stood patiently beside the bed, wagging her tail while the boy rubbed her ears.

"Daisy is the best dog ever," the boy said. "Good dog, Daisy. Good girl."

A woman—probably the boy's mother—watched with tears in her eyes. "Thank you for coming," she told the volunteer. "This is the first time Johnny has smiled since he got here." She patted the golden retriever. "Thank you, too, Daisy," she said.

I finished the second floor, and took the elevator to the fourth floor. That turned out to be the surgical unit and Intensive Care. Instead of individual rooms, the patients were in large rooms, screened from each other by privacy curtains but all open to view from the nurses' station. No visitors were allowed unless they checked in first and only immediate family could enter.

I returned to the lobby to wait for Lauren.

"No sign of her," Lauren said, "but I got to see the new babies in the nursery."

We each had one floor left to do, so we rode the elevator together. Lauren got out on the fifth floor, while I went up to six.

I'd passed only two rooms when I recognized Chance, Jelly Bean's brother. He was sitting up in bed and had no other visitors, so I went in.

"Hi, Chance. How are you doing?"

"Better. I still don't know what happened, but at least I can talk now."

"You can't remember the accident?"

"Nope. I remember I was going to the basketball game, but then my mind goes blank."

"Were you texting?"

Chance gave me a sharp look, and didn't answer.

"I wondered because you were texting and driving while I was in the car and I almost told you it's illegal to do that, but I was afraid you'd get mad and not deliver the food for us again."

Chance still didn't say anything.

I gazed out the window. "I've felt guilty ever since I heard about the accident. I should have spoken up. I should have asked you to stop."

When Chance spoke, his voice was so low I had to strain to hear the words. "The accident wasn't your fault," he said. "It was mine. You're right; I was texting while I drove. The cops haven't talked to me about that yet, but they took my cell phone so they'll be able to tell."

He pounded one fist onto the bed, making me jump. "How could I have been so stupid? I knew it isn't legal to text and drive, but I thought I was such a good driver that I could get away with it. I figured nothing would ever happen to me."

"But it did happen to you."

"It sure did. Not only to me but also to my brother. Because of my stupidity, Jelly Bean has a broken leg and my parents' car insurance cost will zoom skyward, and I'll probably lose my driver's license. You know what the worst part is?"

"What?"

"I'll have to admit to my parents what happened. They're going to find out anyway, so I'll have to tell them the truth."

Even though Chance had caused the accident, he was so miserable now that I felt sorry for him.

"It could have been worse," I said. "Jelly Bean might have been killed."

Chance groaned, as if he couldn't stand to think of that possibility. Then he said, "There's one piece of good news. Jelly Bean had an X-ray this morning and his leg is healing faster than expected."

"That's great. I hope you feel better soon."

"Thanks for coming to visit me," Chance said.

I hurried through the rest of the sixth floor and then met Lauren again.

"No sign of Sophie," Lauren said.

"I didn't see her, either. I wish I'd met Sophie's mother. I might have walked right past her room and didn't know it was her because I don't know what she looks like."

"Let's go look for Sophie in the hospital cafeteria," Lauren said.

We each bought lemonade, but we didn't see Sophie.

"I don't know how else to try to find her," Lauren said.

"Let's find out which school the kids in her neighborhood attend. We could go there and say we're friends of Sophie's and give her address. Even if there's more than one Sophie enrolled, they'd know by the address which one we want. Maybe the school has a contact number."

"Great idea!" Lauren said. "We can do that tomorrow."

It's a good thing I got home before Mom did, because Midnight had knocked over the basket where Mom keeps her knitting and had played with the yarn. Mom was making a blue baby sweater for a coworker's baby shower. Luckily, the stitches were all still on the needle, but the ball of yarn was partially unwound and lying in loops and twists on the floor.

I untangled the mess, rewound the yarn, and put the knitting basket inside the cabinet where Mom keeps it when she isn't working on a project.

I put the rose in a vase and set it on the table. Having a gift for Mom made me feel slightly less guilty about all the things I hadn't told her.

When Mom got home she said, "Where did the rose come from?"

"It's for you," I said. "I bought it."

"Thank you, Emmy," she said, and gave me a big hug. I was startled to see tears in her eyes, and I promised myself I would try harder to do nice things for Mom. Seeing how much she appreciated the rose made me feel even worse about not telling her what I'd been doing.

I wanted to tell her about the hospital, about visiting Chance and about the service dog who made a sick boy smile, but I couldn't do that without explaining why I had gone there.

CHAPTER NINE

Lauren called early the next morning. "I'm sick," she said. "I'm staying in bed today, so I can't go with you to Sophie's school this afternoon."

"What's wrong with you?"

"Sore throat, and I'm running a fever. Mom thinks I might have strep."

"Drink a lot of water," I said. "I hope you're better soon."

That afternoon as I boarded the city bus, headed for Sophie's school, I wondered why I felt responsible for helping Sophie. Except for Lauren, the other kids in my group had felt good about doing a community service project and had then shrugged, said it was not their problem, and let it go. They weren't spending their afternoons riding buses and leaning into Dumpsters and walking hospital corridors, looking into the rooms of strangers. They weren't talking to No Help and worrying that they might get rabies. They had put Sophie's troubles out of their minds and gone on to concentrate on trying out for the school play or learning to do wheelies on a skateboard. Why couldn't I be like that? Why did I have to care so much?

I did not have to transfer to a second bus to get to Sophie's school, but I did have to walk ten blocks from the bus stop. I reached the building and went inside. School was out for the day, so the halls were empty.

A woman in a purple blouse looked up from her keyboard when I entered the office. A bouquet of fake red roses sat on her desk along with a framed photograph of a white poodle wearing a yellow raincoat.

"What can I do for you?" she asked.

"A girl I know goes to this school," I said. "She lost her cat and I found it, but I don't know her last name so I can't look up her phone number. Her first name is Sophie, and I hope you can tell me her last name."

"I can't give out student information," she said. "District rule."

"I know it's a rule," I said, "but I also know she's worried sick about her cat." I wanted to add that there are far too many rules that make it hard to help people, but I didn't. Instead I said, "Sophie's mom is sick and her dad is gone and she's having a really hard time right now. Midnight, her cat, means the world to her."

The woman nodded. "There's more than one Sophie in this school," she said.

"The one I want lives on East Sycamore Street."

"If you know where she lives, why don't you take the cat to her? Or go there and talk to her?"

"I did go there, but nobody's home. The last time I talked to Sophie, her mom was in the hospital and Sophie was staying with someone else."

The woman typed something and I saw new information come up on her computer screen, but she didn't say anything. She seemed to be thinking over my request.

I said, "How would you feel if your dog was lost and somebody found it, but they didn't know how to get hold of you to let you know he was okay?"

The woman glanced briefly at the poodle picture on her desk.

"What grade is your friend in?" she asked.

"Fifth."

She clicked a few keys.

"I heard there might be a Sophie Sodaberg in the fifth grade," she said, "but I can't confirm that."

"Thanks," I said.

I had been afraid Sophie's last name might be Smith or Johnson or some other common name. How many Sodabergs could there be in Cedar Hill?

The walk back to the bus stop seemed shorter than the walk to the school.

As soon as I got home, I called the hospital.

"I'm calling about Mrs. Sodaberg," I said. "She's a patient

there and I'd like to know her room number so I can send her some flowers."

"One moment, please."

I held my breath. If I got the room number for Sophie's mom, I could go there and find Sophie. Or if Sophie wasn't visiting when I got there, I could tell her mom about Midnight, or even leave a note for Sophie at the nurses' station.

"Hello?" the voice came back on the line. "Mrs. Sodaberg is no longer a patient here. She was discharged last night."

"Oh," I said. "Okay. Thank you."

Discharged! Instead of going to Sophie's school, I should have gone back to her apartment. She was probably there, calling and hunting for Midnight.

Mom would be home soon; it was too late to go to Sophie's apartment.

The next day was the last day of school before spring break. Mrs. Reed gave one of her "let's make the world a better place" talks and had each of us say one thing we could do every day that would make us better people. We were supposed to put our resolutions into practice during our vacation from school.

Hunter said, "I'm going to make my bed every day so I don't get docked on my allowance."

Shoeless said, "I'm going to learn how to make deep-fried Oreos."

"Resolutions are supposed to make you a better person," Mrs. Reed said.

"I'll be lots better if I can have deep-fried Oreos whenever I want them," Shoeless said.

Crystal said, "I'm going to volunteer with a group that catches aliens and puts tracking devices on them so the FBI knows where they are."

"Where do you find aliens?" asked Abby.

"Oh, I can't tell you that," Crystal said. "They are not aware that we know where they're hiding, so it has to be kept a secret."

"Yeah, right," said Shoeless.

"Next, please," said Mrs. Reed.

Most of the resolutions were typical: be nice to my little brother, do my homework on time, get up when the alarm rings. I resolved to keep my room clean without being nagged.

That afternoon we had an assembly where the school band played some of the songs they'd be playing in the concert.

Usually by that point on the last day before spring break I was giddy with anticipation and full of plans for all my free time.

This year, I shivered as I waited for the city bus to take me to Sophie's apartment. Lauren was still home sick, so I was alone. I didn't really want to make this trip again, but Sophie needed to know that Midnight was safe. If she was living in the apartment again, I could return Midnight to her. Not on the bus, though.

I climbed the familiar stairs to apartment 3 and knocked. No answer. I knocked harder. Silence.

As I debated what to do next, I heard the outside door open and close. Hoping it was Sophie, I looked down the stairs.

No Help approached, carrying a can of beer.

"Oh, it's you again," he said.

"I'm looking for Sophie," I said.

"She isn't there. They've all left."

"What do you mean?"

"I mean they've moved out. Evacuated the premises."

"That's what you said before, but it wasn't true. Sophie's mom was in the hospital."

"They all came home yesterday, and last night they left again carrying suitcases. This time they're gone for good. I know because your friend knocked on my door and said they were moving, and asked if I had seen her cat."

"What did you tell her?"

"I said no."

I glared at him. "You didn't tell her you had thrown the cat in the Dumpster?"

"How did you . . ." He clamped his mouth shut.

"I should report you for animal cruelty," I said.

"Your word against mine," he said. "You have no proof."

He unlocked the door to his apartment, went inside, and shut the door.

I tried to think what I would do if I were Sophie and had to leave my cat behind when I moved. I decided I would leave an address or phone number with my neighbors, in case anyone saw Midnight.

I knocked on No Help's door. No response. I banged louder.

"Go away!"

"I need to talk to you."

The door opened slightly.

"Make it fast; I'm busy."

"Did Sophie give you a phone number, in case you saw her cat?"

"Forget the cat. It's gone."

"Did she give you a phone number or not?"

"Yeah, yeah. She gave me a number."

"Could I please have it?"

"Nope."

"Why not? What difference does it make to you?"

"I don't have it."

"You said she gave it to you!"

"She told it to me, and I pretended to write it down."

"Pretended."

"I knew nobody would see that cat hanging around so why bother?"

I stared at him. I realized he thought nobody would see Midnight because he believed Midnight was dead in the Dumpster. He made me so mad that I wanted to get even somehow.

"When you threw Midnight in the Dumpster," I said, "you might as well have tossed in a handful of hundred-dollar bills."

"What are you talking about?"

He opened the door a little farther.

I looked past him into his apartment and saw a whole row of flat-screen TVs.

"Don't get nosy!" No Help said. "If you come here again, you'll wish you hadn't."

This time when he slammed the door, I heard the lock click into place.

Why would No Help have so many television sets? Why didn't he want me to see them?

CHAPTER TEN

I banged on No Help's door and shouted, "There's a one-thousand-dollar reward for the return of that cat!"

The door opened. No Help looked out. "What?" he said.

"Haven't you seen the posters?" I said. "There's a picture of Sophie's cat, and it says there's a one-thousand-dollar reward."

"No way! That family couldn't even pay their bills. Their car got repossessed one day when they weren't home, and someone from the landlord's company had to let them in yesterday because the rent was overdue and he'd already changed the locks. Where would they get a thousand dollars?"

"The reward is from an organization that helps low-income people take care of their pets."

"You're kidding." His eyes opened wider.

"Nope," I said. "One thousand dollars. Cash." I couldn't believe how easily the lies came out of my mouth. I hadn't thought this story up in advance; the words tumbled out spontaneously, and when I saw the effect they had on No Help, I embellished the story. "All you have to do is call the number on the poster and they'll come and get the cat and give you the money."

No Help pushed past me and ran down the stairs. I followed. He rushed to the back of the building, jumped up beside the Dumpster, grabbed the rim and pulled himself up so that he could see inside. "Here, kitty!" he called. "Nice kitty, kitty!"

For an instant I fantasized about grabbing his ankles and shoving him up and over the top. Let him see how he liked sitting in the stinky garbage.

Instead I left him hollering into the Dumpster, while I ran back up the stairs. He had left the door of his apartment partway open. I pushed it open wider and peered inside. I stayed in the hallway, right at the threshold, so I couldn't be accused of trespassing, but I got a good look.

Along with all the TV sets, there were about a dozen laptop computers, and a large open cardboard box full of cell phones. Several boxes stacked on a card table said "Blu-ray" on the side. I took out my phone and snapped some pictures of the room's contents.

I pulled the door closed until it was exactly the way No Help had left it. Then I ran downstairs and knocked on Mrs. Spangler's door. Maybe Sophie had asked her to watch for Midnight, and Mrs. Spangler would have told her how I fished him out of the Dumpster and took him home. If that had happened, I could relax about the whole situation. Sophie wouldn't worry about Midnight, and she could contact me when she was settled in her new home, wherever that might be. Of course, I still had to convince Mom to let me keep Midnight until I talked to Sophie.

It took a few minutes for Mrs. Spangler to answer my knock. When she saw me her face crinkled into a smile.

"It's the cat girl," she said. "Come in! How's the kitty doing?"

"He's fine," I said. "He gets along great with my dog."

"We humans could learn a lot from the creatures about how to live happily with those who are different from ourselves," she said. "We surely could. Would you like some hot chocolate?"

"No, thanks. I can't stay. Did Sophie, the girl who lived upstairs, talk to you about her cat before she left?"

"Left? Have they moved out?"

"Yes. At least that's what the man upstairs in apartment four told me."

"Oh, him. I wouldn't trust anything that comes out of that one's mouth."

"Do you know what his name is?" When I told the police about all the electronics that were stashed in No Help's living room, it would be good if I knew his name.

She shook her head, no. "I don't know his name, but I know he's rude. More than once I've heard him shout at someone in his apartment. He has a foul mouth."

"He's the one who threw Sophie's cat in the Dumpster," I said.

"I'm not surprised," Mrs. Spangler said. "Once I heard a commotion, and when I looked out, a man had fallen on the stairs. That neighbor stood at the top laughing, as if it was funny that someone had tripped on the stairs. He made no effort to help the man who had fallen. I wondered if he might have pushed the man. I probably should have called the police, but I didn't actually see what happened. All I know for sure is that he has a mean streak."

"He's a jerk, but I think he's right about Sophie's family moving. I hoped you might have seen Sophie before she left, and told her that I rescued Midnight from the Dumpster and took him home."

"I wish I'd had a chance to do that," Mrs. Spangler said. "I surely do. I would have enjoyed telling that story to someone, but I haven't talked to anybody. No one has been here since you came before."

Maybe she didn't hear Sophie knock, I thought. Or maybe Sophie's mother hurried her along and wouldn't wait while Sophie talked to Mrs. Spangler.

I thanked Mrs. Spangler and said I'd come back to visit her on a day when I could stay longer. When I went outside I heard No Help banging his fists on the side of the Dumpster, probably trying to scare poor Midnight into moving around so he could see him. I wondered how long he would bang and yell before he gave up.

I walked back to the bus stop, feeling like a failure. Sophie was gone. I hadn't told her I have Midnight and now I might never see her again, and she would always wonder what had happened to her little black cat. Sophie had enough problems without grieving for a cat who was safe and happy.

A tear trickled down my cheek. I had tried so hard to help, but all I did was waste a bunch of time and get a zillion scratches.

I had to wait ten minutes for the bus. Just as it pulled up, I saw No Help come out to the front of his building. He started toward me as I got on the bus. The doors closed. I quickly dropped my fare in the container and found an empty seat. I vowed I would never come back here again.

The bus started to pull away from the curb, then stopped. The front door creaked open, and No Help got on. His eyes scanned the rows of seats until he saw me. Then he dropped his fare in the coin box, walked up the aisle, and sat beside me.

"What are you up to?" he asked.

"I don't know what you mean."

"I mean why did you knock on my door?"

"I told you why. I'm looking for Sophie."

"Where are those posters?" he asked. "I didn't see them."

"They were on telephone poles around the area," I said. "I don't remember exactly where."

"Funny you saw them but I didn't."

"I'm very observant," I said.

"So, what did you observe in my apartment?"

"I've never been inside your apartment."

I grew more and more uneasy. I knew that he'd noticed me looking into his apartment. Was he trying to warn me not to tell anyone what I'd seen?

"You never looked in the door, either. You saw nothing in that room. Right?"

"Right." I gave him my most innocent look. "Was there something in there you wanted me to see?" I asked. "If there was, I missed it."

"I don't know what game you're playing," he said, "but you had better stop it before you get hurt."

I didn't answer. It seemed wiser not to continue to talk to him. For the first time, I wondered if helping Sophie might be dangerous.

We rode in silence until the bus got to my stop. When I got off, No Help got off, too. Fear moved into my mind and took up residence.

I walked quickly toward home. No Help followed. The bus stop is five blocks from my house. No Help didn't say anything, and he didn't try to walk beside me, but he followed me. When I got within a block of my house, I started to run. No Help ran after me. I knew he could catch up to me if he wanted to, but he stayed about fifteen feet back.

When I got to my house he waited on the sidewalk, watching while I opened my front door and went inside. I was glad I had remembered to take my key that day so that I didn't have to get the spare one from under the fake rock where we hide it.

I locked the door behind me, then ran to the window and peered out. No Help had turned and was walking back toward the bus stop. Waggy greeted me as usual, and I knelt beside him and buried my face in his fur, trying to make my heart quit racing. Instead of walking Waggy around the block as I

normally do when I get home, I kept him in our backyard. I
didn't want to take any chance of seeing No Help again.

I had intended to download and print my pictures of his
apartment, write the address on the back, and mail them to
the police as an anonymous tip, but I realized that if the cops
showed up at No Help's door to question him, he would guess
who had alerted them. The tip would be anonymous and No
Help didn't know my name, but he knew where I lived. I didn't
want to give him any excuse to return.

I couldn't prove that anything in his apartment was
stolen. Maybe he ran some kind of business where he bought
inexpensive or damaged electronics and resold them for a
profit. If that was the case, though, he wouldn't care if I saw
the items. He would have no reason to threaten me.

Why had he followed me home? The only possible answer
was that he wanted to scare me, to warn me not to tell anyone
what I had seen.

I called Lauren and told her that Sophie's family was gone,
but I didn't tell her about No Help. Since I wasn't going to do
anything with those pictures, it would be best if nobody else
knew about them, or about my being followed.

"I wish I'd never read that contest entry," I said. "I've
wasted tons of time, and I have nothing to show for my efforts."

"That isn't true," Lauren said. "You helped Sophie's family
when they desperately needed food. You rescued Midnight. He
would have died in that Dumpster if it hadn't been for you.
Even though the situation isn't ending the way you had hoped
it would, you still accomplished a lot."

Her words made me feel better.

"I think you'll hear from Sophie again," Lauren said.

"Seriously?"

"You don't know how to contact her, but she knows how to reach you."

"No, she doesn't. If she had found the note with my phone number, she would have called. She doesn't know my address or even my last name. It would be as hard for her to contact me as it is for me to find her."

"Maybe not. She could send another letter to Dunbar's. Once she gets settled wherever she's gone, I bet she'll figure out a way to get in touch with you to let you know she's okay. When she does, you can tell her you have Midnight and make arrangements to get him back to her."

I hoped Lauren was right. I felt better thinking that I might eventually hear from Sophie again.

When Mom got home, she began reading contest entries. "This will be the last batch until next year," she said. "Yesterday was the deadline, and I thought I was through, but Colleen found a pile of entries that had fallen down behind her desk."

I went to my room and started my homework.

A few minutes later, Mom came in. She had that "You are in big trouble, young lady" look in her eye as she handed me an envelope.

I knew before I read it what it was.

CHAPTER ELEVEN

I read Sophie's letter slowly, trying to decide what to say. It would be pointless to lie. Mom has an uncanny way of knowing if I am stretching the truth.

The letter said:

> Dear Dunbar's, Thank you for the bags of food. They helped us a lot. When I wrote my entry for your contest, I didn't expect to win, but I didn't know who else to ask for help. Trudy goes right to sleep now that she isn't hungry. I'm happy to have cat food, too. Thank you for your kindness. Sophie

I handed the letter back to Mom.
"Well?" she said.

I was tired of hiding my actions. I'd been skulking around like a secret spy, trying to disguise my efforts to help Sophie, and now she was gone, anyway. No matter how much trouble I got in, and I knew Mom would not be pleased, I decided to tell the truth.

I told Mom everything—how I'd shown Sophie's entry to my classmates, how we'd all collected food, how Chance had driven Jelly Bean and me to Sophie's house to deliver it.

"You knew you were risking my job," Mom said.

"I wasn't! That's why I didn't tell you. If you didn't know what we were doing, it wouldn't be your fault and Dunbar's couldn't fire you."

Mom sighed and closed her eyes.

"I'm sorry, Mom," I said, "but I couldn't let those kids be hungry."

She looked at me again. "I'm glad you have a tender heart, Emmy," she said. "I want you to be the kind of person who cares about those who are less fortunate, but there's a right way and a wrong way to help others. This was the wrong way."

"Sophie's family was hungry," I said. "Because of the food we took them, Trudy doesn't cry herself to sleep anymore. How can that be wrong?"

I could tell Mom wasn't really angry over what I'd done; she was upset that I hadn't been honest about it.

"Sophie is a nice girl," I said. "She's two years younger than I am, and she loves animals."

"You met her? Her thank-you note doesn't mention that."

"I met her twice, but not until after she wrote this letter.

The first time was when we took the second load of groceries, the day Chance had his accident."

"The second load? You went there more than once?"

I nodded, staring at my shoes.

"Which means you rode with Chance more than one time."

"Yes. The accident happened after we went the second time."

"Where does this Sophie live?"

"On East Sycamore Street. It's near the gravel pit."

"That's clear on the other side of town," she said. "How long did you intend to keep doing this?"

"Not much longer. Abby and Shoeless went to the food bank to find out what Sophie's mother needs to do in order to get food there. I told Sophie what to do and, as soon as her mother gets well, Sophie is going to tell her."

Mom's expression softened a little. "The mother is sick?"

"She had pneumonia. The last time I saw Sophie was at the hospital when I went with Mrs. Reed to visit Jelly Bean. I wanted to introduce Sophie to Mrs. Reed, but Sophie wouldn't let me, and she asked me not to tell anyone about her mom. She said there are things I don't know about her family, and I'd only make it worse if I try to get help for them."

"What about Sophie's father?"

"All she said was her dad's gone, and they might have to go back to Mexico to live with her grandparents."

"This is not a problem that can be solved by a group of sixth-grade kids," Mom said. "I'll call the state social services agency tomorrow and ask them to get aid for Sophie's family."

"It's too late. They moved out yesterday, and I don't know where they went."

"How do you know they've moved?"

"Their next-door neighbor told me. He saw them leave, carrying suitcases, and he said Sophie had told him they were moving."

"If they moved yesterday," Mom said slowly, "it means you talked to the neighbor last night or today."

I nodded.

"So, when did you get this information?"

"Today," I said.

"How did you get to Sophie's apartment?"

"I took the bus."

"The bus."

I nodded again.

"By yourself? That area by the gravel pit is no place for you to be waiting alone for a bus."

"The first time I took the bus there, Lauren went with me."

"The first time." Mom repeated my words as if she needed a translator.

"Right. Lauren and I collected bags of food from her neighbors and delivered them on the bus."

"You took food there again? After Chance's accident?"

"Sophie and Trudy were still hungry. Chance being hospitalized didn't change that."

"If you had let me know about Sophie's family," Mom said, "I might have been able to find help for them."

"I did tell you, when I first read Sophie's contest entry.

You said Help Your Neighbor was almost out of money and there wasn't anything you could do."

"You're right." Mom spoke slowly. "You read the entry to me the day I had the flu. Your dad was out of town, and I already felt as if I couldn't handle all my problems, but I was wrong to ignore Sophie's situation. There are many social service agencies and churches with programs to assist families like Sophie's. If I had sought help from one of them, perhaps Sophie would not have had to move."

"You said you would lose your job if you did that."

"I could have talked to my supervisor and explained the situation. Mrs. Murphy is not a hard-hearted person. There might have been a way to bend the rules, maybe by finding some other nonprofit group that would help."

That possibility made me feel sick. Instead of hiding my actions, I should have admitted what I was doing and asked for advice. Maybe Mom could have found a way to help Sophie's family that would have allowed them to stay where they were. Instead Sophie had left her home, her school, her cat—and maybe even her country.

"If Sophie hadn't written to thank Dunbar's, I would never have found out about this," Mom said.

"Dunbar's didn't find out, either," I said. "It didn't affect your job at all."

"That doesn't mean you're off the hook. I feel sorry for Sophie and her family, but the fact remains that you deliberately did something you had been told not to do."

"I'm sorry. I didn't like going behind your back, but I didn't know what else to do."

"It was dangerous!" Mom said. "You rode with an inexperienced driver. You went alone into an area that's known for its high crime rate. You're lucky you didn't get mugged!"

"When you put it that way, I feel stupid. I only wanted to help Sophie's family."

"Well, it's over now," Mom said, "and you're safe." She opened her arms to give me a hug.

I hugged her, and then stepped back. "There's one more thing I need to tell you," I said.

Mom rolled her eyes as if wondering why she was burdened with me for a daughter.

"Midnight is Sophie's cat," I said.

"What? Why did you bring him home?"

"Sophie kept him inside her apartment, but when Lauren and I took the third load of food over there nobody was home and Midnight was meowing in the hallway outside her apartment. We think he escaped when the ambulance came for Sophie's mom. When her mom had to stay at the hospital, Sophie and Trudy went to stay with someone else and they couldn't get home to take care of Midnight, and then the next time I went . . ."

"The next time? When was this?"

"The day Lauren had to go to the dentist. I went by myself and that's when I heard Midnight crying because their mean neighbor had thrown him in the Dumpster."

"So you did rescue him from a Dumpster. I'm glad you told me at least part of what you had done."

"A lady named Mrs. Spangler helped me get him out. She let me use her step stool and a laundry basket."

"How did you meet her?"

"She lives downstairs in Sophie's building. I knocked on her door and asked if I could borrow a ladder."

"You were alone, in a neighborhood where you didn't know anyone, and you knocked on the door of a complete stranger?"

When she said it like that, it didn't sound like the smartest move I'd ever made.

"Mrs. Spangler uses a walker and moves slowly, and she's really nice. She gave me a can of tuna for bait so Midnight would get in the basket."

"Instead of a kindly old woman, that door could have been opened by a serial killer."

I ignored that remark because, really, what could I say? She was right. The door could have been opened by a nutcase with a gun who hated kids, or by a whole gang of hoodlums. Instead of defending my actions, I told her what had happened.

"After I got Midnight out, I smuggled him home on the bus."

Mom seemed stunned. "I wonder if a nurse accidentally switched my baby with someone else's baby when you were born," she said.

"Mom!"

"I can't believe all of this has been going on and I didn't know anything about it."

Suddenly she started to laugh. "You have to admit this is a pretty wild story."

"It sure is."

It was a wild story, and Mom didn't even know all of it. She had already expressed so many worries about what might have happened to me that I knew she'd totally freak out if I told her that No Help had followed me home, so I didn't tell her. That information would only prove how wrong I had been to go there alone, and make her paranoid about letting me go anywhere by myself ever again. If Mom knew about No Help, she would guard me like the Secret Service.

If I never returned to East Sycamore Street, and didn't tell anyone what I'd seen in No Help's apartment, he would forget about me and the whole thing would fade away. The best course of action was inaction.

"Have you written to Sophie, to tell her that you have Midnight?" Mom asked.

"Where would I send it? I don't have her new address."

"Mail it to the old address," Mom said. "If you write *Please forward* on the envelope, the Post Office will send it to her new address, if they have one."

"That's a great idea!" I said. "Thanks, Mom."

"We aren't done discussing this," Mom said. "I will need to talk to your father."

I nodded. The explanation of how I had helped Sophie seemed worse when it was told all at one time than it had when one little part happened, and then another part, and then one more. Each time I'd gone to Sophie's house, I had thought it would be my last trip there. Because I always believed the whole project would soon be over, the individual events never seemed like a huge deal. One day to ride with Chance or one day to take the bus or one visit to Sophie's school didn't seem too wrong, but each action became a link that, when put together, made a long chain of deceit and bad decisions.

CHAPTER TWELVE

Lauren called the next afternoon. "Jelly Bean's brother went home from the hospital," she said. "I saw it on his CaringBridge page. It says he's expected to make a full recovery."

"That's great news."

My grandparents came to visit during my spring break, so Mom and Dad both took a few days of vacation and we did touristy things in the Puget Sound area. We watched boats go through the Ballard Locks, we browsed through Pike Place Market, and we spent an afternoon admiring the cars in the LeMay Museum.

After one of our outings, we ate dinner at Burger Barn and Grandma noticed that I ordered a salad instead of the burger, fries, and strawberry milk shake that I used to get.

"I feel better when I eat healthy food," I explained.

"You look good, too," Grandma said.

I knew I'd lost a few pounds because my jeans were loose, but I hadn't thought it was noticeable to other people.

Sitting in Burger Barn, I realized the restaurant might yield a possible clue that I had not pursued.

"Sophie's mom worked at Burger Barn before she got sick," I told Mom. "Maybe some of the employees know her."

Mom asked to speak to the manager and when he came over, she explained that we were trying to find a woman who used to work at Burger Barn. "We don't know her first name but her last name is Sodaberg."

He shook his head. "That doesn't ring any bells," he said. "How long ago did she work here?"

"Until about three weeks ago," I said. "Then she got sick."

"Are you sure she worked at this Burger Barn? There are two others in Cedar Hill."

"We'll try them," Mom said. "Thanks for your help."

I wanted to drive to the other two Burger Barns right then, but Mom said she would call them when we got home. "This can be handled by phone," she said. I think she didn't want to do too much explaining to Grandpa and Grandma about how I had become involved with Sophie's family.

After we got home, Mom called the other two Burger Barns and spoke to both of the managers, but she didn't find anyone who knew Sophie's mother. One of the managers said she was new on the job and didn't know any former employees. Mom told the managers that she was trying to return the family cat to Mrs. Sodaberg's daughters, hoping that would jog someone's memory, but Burger Barn was another dead end.

"Maybe Sophie's mother's name isn't Sodaberg," Mom said. "Parents and kids don't always have the same last name."

After Grandma and Grandpa went home, Lauren came for a sleepover and then school started again. On our first day back, Mrs. Reed had each of us tell the best thing that we had done during vacation.

Jelly Bean was back in class, using crutches. Signatures and drawings now covered his whole cast. He said, "My best thing is that my brother came home from the hospital."

Crystal waved her hand wildly, trying to get Mrs. Reed to call on her. I thought she would talk about aliens, but when it was her turn she said, "I saw a Sasquatch! I found its tracks and followed them along the edge of a creek."

"Where was this?" Mrs. Reed asked.

"In Victory Creek Park."

Here she goes again, I thought. Reports of a Sasquatch, or Bigfoot, had surfaced for years in Washington State with some people believing the large furry animal/person was real and others convinced it was a myth or a hoax. Sasquatches were usually reported deep in the woods, far from populated areas.

Victory Creek Park is a small city park that has a playground and a few picnic tables. One side abuts the parking lot of a large grocery store. The chances of a Sasquatch, if there are such creatures, in that area seemed unlikely and if there had been one, surely Crystal would not be the only person to notice it.

Mrs. Reed opened her mouth as if to dispute what Crystal had said, then hesitated and said, "Next, please," and Hunter told about visiting the Museum of History and Industry.

When it was Abby's turn, she said, "I can tell a best thing but I also have a worst thing that happened."

"Go ahead," said Mrs. Reed.

"The best thing was that I got a laptop computer from my parents for my birthday. It was the only thing I really wanted, but I didn't expect to get it. I was thrilled when I unwrapped that gift. I spent the next five days on it. I opened an e-mail account, and I surfed all kinds of interesting websites and watched funny videos on YouTube."

She paused. Her bottom lip trembled and tears pooled in her eyes. "Then the worst thing happened." Her voice dropped almost to a whisper, as if she had to force herself to say the words. "Someone broke into our house while we were at a movie and stole my laptop."

There was a collective "Oh," as the class reacted to Abby's news.

"The burglar took our TV, too, which was almost new, and the Blu-ray player that my parents gave each other last Christmas. My dad had left some cash in his desk drawer, and it was gone."

"Did you call the police?" Lauren asked.

"Yes. The police came and made a list of everything that was missing, but they didn't hold out much hope that we would get any of it back. The officers said there's been a rash of home burglaries in Cedar Hill in the last few months. Most of what's been stolen has been new or nearly new electronics.

They suspect it's some kind of professional ring that has a fast and efficient way to get rid of the stolen items."

"My aunt's house was burglarized, too," Hunter said. "Someone broke in while she was at work and stole her computer and her TV and her new camera. The computer had personal information on it and the thief got her credit card and bank account numbers. Aunt Karen found out about the theft when the credit card company called her because a bunch of stuff that wasn't the kind of thing she usually buys had been charged on her card, and they wanted to be sure she was the buyer. She hadn't bought any of it."

As I looked at Abby's tearful face and heard what had happened to Hunter's aunt, I thought about No Help's apartment full of TVs, computers, and other electronic merchandise. What if he was the thief? Maybe he was part of the ring that the police suspected was operating in the area. Stolen goods might be stashed at his apartment while he advertised them for sale on eBay or craigslist. Maybe right at that minute Abby's new laptop was sitting in apartment 4 of the building on East Sycamore Street.

I still had the photos of his apartment on my phone. Even though I had not shown them to anyone, I hadn't deleted them. Now I decided that I couldn't keep that information to myself any longer. If I had a clue or evidence that might help solve the burglaries, I needed to give it to the police.

Instead of going straight home after school that day, I went to the Cedar Hill police station. It's next door to the post office, so I had been past the building many times, but I had never gone inside before. As I climbed the concrete steps and pulled open the front door, my mouth felt dry, and I glanced back toward the street to see if anyone was watching me.

An information counter stood inside the door. A thick Plexiglas shield rose from the top of the counter toward the ceiling. It looked like the ticket window at a movie theater, with just enough room between the bottom of the window and the counter to slide your money in and get the tickets back.

I didn't see a person, but there was a round silver bell with a sign that said RING FOR SERVICE. I tapped the bell, and it dinged. A uniformed officer appeared on the other side of the window.

"I'm Lieutenant Benson," she said. "What can I do for you?"

"I was looking for a friend's missing cat," I said, "and I knocked on her neighbor's door. When he answered, I saw a whole lot of TVs and computers in his apartment. It seemed odd for one person to have so many. Then at school today my friend said her laptop and her family's TV got stolen, and another classmate said his aunt's house was burglarized and the thief took her computer. I wonder if maybe the apartment full of electronics that I saw is connected to the burglaries."

"It's possible."

"When the man went downstairs and left his door open, I took a couple of pictures." I found the first photo on my phone and passed the phone under the glass to Lieutenant Benson.

"There are two more pictures," I said. "Hit the down arrow."

She did. "Where were these taken?" she asked.

I gave her the address and she wrote it down.

"Who lives there?"

"I don't know his name. My friend used to live in the apartment next to his, but she's moved away."

"Is it all right if I download these pictures?"

"Yes. That's why I came; I want you to have them."

I waited while she hooked up my phone to her computer and downloaded the three pictures.

She gave me back my phone. "Have you shown these pictures to anyone?"

"No."

"Does the man who lives there know you took them?"

"No. He was out in back banging on the Dumpster because he thought there was a reward for Sophie's cat."

"Do you live with your parents?" she asked.

"Yes."

"Do they know you're here?"

"No. They don't know about the man or the pictures."

Lieutenant Benson raised her eyebrows as if to say, Oh? Why not?

"It's kind of complicated," I said. "I already got in trouble for going to Sophie's house alone, and it would be worse if my parents found out I had met this man and photographed his living room. I had decided not to show the pictures to anyone but when Abby told how her house was burglarized and the thief stole her new laptop, she was crying and I felt sorry for her. I realized by not turning in my pictures, I might be helping whoever stole from Abby get away with it. I want them to get caught. I want Abby to get her laptop back."

"We'll want to pursue this," Lieutenant Benson said. "I'm glad you decided to bring in your pictures—and I think it would be a good idea for you to tell your parents exactly what you've told me."

She gave me a form to fill out: name, address, phone, the reason I was there, and permission for the police department to download the photos. I decided to use my middle name so I wrote Louise Rushford. If my tip worked, and they caught the burglar, a nosy reporter might learn who the anonymous informant was, and publish that information. I felt safer not giving my full name.

There was a section for minors to list the names and addresses of their parents. I wondered if Mom and Dad would learn about the pictures whether I told them or not. If Mom got a call from a police officer who said she was calling about me, Mom would have an anxiety attack for sure, and I'd be grounded for the rest of my life, but it was too late to back out now.

I filled in the rest of the form accurately, signed it Louise Rushford, and gave it back. "What will happen now?" I asked.

"We'll find out who lives at the address where you took the photos. We'll go there and have a talk with him."

"Maybe he has a legitimate reason to have all that equipment. Maybe he's running a business," I said.

"Maybe." Lieutenant Benson did not seem convinced of that.

I wasn't, either. Someone who did not have paper and a pencil did not seem a likely candidate to be running his own small business, and if the items in his apartment had been legitimately for sale, he would not have tried to hide them from me.

"Actually, the man is a slime ball," I said. "He threw Sophie's cat in the Dumpster. If I hadn't heard Midnight meowing and rescued him, he would have died."

"That's animal cruelty," Lieutenant Benson said. "If you want to file a complaint, we might be able to charge him on that, too."

"I can't prove that he's the one who threw Midnight in the Dumpster, although he admitted that he did it. I really don't want him to find out that I alerted you. He won't know I turned in these photos because he doesn't know I took them, but if I file an animal cruelty complaint, he'll know it came from me." I tried not to think about the fact that, although No Help didn't know I had taken the pictures, he did know I had looked in the door of his apartment. And he knew where I lived.

Lieutenant Benson nodded. "Thanks for bringing your pictures, Louise," she said. "They might be the break we need on a lot of burglary cases."

As I left the police station, I felt good about what I had done. All the way home I debated whether to tell Mom and Dad about the pictures. On the one hand, I was already in hot water for not telling my parents about a problem. If I kept this information secret, and they later found out about it, I would be in even worse trouble with them.

On the other hand, I had turned my evidence over to the police and I did not intend to have anything more to do with the matter, so what would be gained by getting Mom and Dad all worked up now? My involvement in the case was over.

Or so I thought.

CHAPTER THIRTEEN

My letter to Sophie came back with the envelope stamped "No forwarding address. Return to sender."

How can three people disappear without a trace? It seemed as if someone, somewhere, must know how to reach Sophie's family if I could only figure out who that someone was.

The next day I listened to local news, traffic, and weather on the kitchen radio while I fixed breakfast. As I poured milk on my cereal, I heard the announcer say, "A suspect was arrested in Cedar Hill last night on multiple burglary charges. Police believe Donald Zummer may be responsible for more than twenty local residential burglaries in the last two months. An anonymous tip led them to his apartment on East Sycamore Street, which was filled with stolen items. When the suspect answered the door, officers served him with a search warrant, which led to Zummer's arrest. He will be arraigned today at nine a.m. in District Court."

I pumped my fist in the air. An anonymous tip! That was me! No Help had been arrested because of the pictures I took.

I was bursting to share this news but since no one knew what I'd seen in No Help's apartment, or that I had taken pictures, or that I had given the photos to the police, there wasn't anyone who would understand my excitement.

Mom was upstairs getting ready for work. I hoped if she heard the news report on the car radio she would not remember that Sophie had lived on East Sycamore.

I didn't want to confirm that danger lurked in the neighborhood where I'd gone alone.

As soon as I got to school, I told Abby about the news report. "Maybe it's the person who broke into your house," I said. "Maybe the police will recover your laptop and you'll get it back."

"That would be so cool," she said.

Seeing her smile and the hope in her eyes made me doubly glad that I had turned in those pictures. I hugged the secret to myself the whole day.

I watched the TV news that night, but there had been a terrible tornado in Oklahoma that killed twenty-four people so any story about a local burglar got bumped in favor of storm-chaser video and grim photos of flattened buildings. I wondered what had happened during No Help's court appearance, but I didn't know how to find out.

The next day before class started I asked Abby if her family had heard anything more from the police.

"My dad called Lieutenant Benson, the police officer who is working on our case," she said. "The suspect pleaded not guilty and was released on twenty-thousand-dollars' bail. Dad asked about our stolen things. The police need to photograph all the items, and record and check serial numbers. Then they release the property to the victims as quickly as possible. Lieutenant Benson said she would call as soon as she knew if any of what they retrieved belonged to us." Abby smiled. "We thought our things were gone for good and we didn't know where." Like Sophie, I thought. She's gone for good, and I don't know where.

"Now," Abby said, "I might get my laptop back."

Class began. Mrs. Reed showed us a film about the planets. Ordinarily, I would be interested in astronomy but that day my mind kept wandering back to Sophie, trying to think of some way to contact her.

After recess, Mrs. Reed told us that our school would be participating in a Career Day event at the high school. "Please ask your parents if they might be willing to speak for ten minutes about their career," she said. "We especially need people in the medical field, and an attorney."

"Will there be a landlord?" asked Crystal.

"I don't think any real estate investors are represented," Mrs. Reed said. "Do your parents own rental property?"

"They don't own it. They rent it, and if our landlord will be there, I'm not going. My aunt and uncle moved out of the unit next to ours, and the landlord won't give them back their damage deposit because he says their sixteen cats ruined the carpet. That carpet was a wreck before they ever moved in, and the fridge never worked right, and my uncle's going to sue the landlord for ten million dollars and when he wins, he'll give some of it to me, and . . ."

"Thank you, Crystal," said Mrs. Reed. "Class, please open your math books to page sixty."

Usually I tuned out when Crystal got off on one of her rants, but this time I felt like cheering. Crystal had given me a great idea.

I asked Lauren if she still had the phone number for the company that owned the apartment where Sophie had lived.

"Why do you want that?" Lauren asked.

"Listening to Crystal talk about her aunt and uncle's cats made me wonder if Sophie's mother had put down a damage deposit when they moved into their apartment. If she did, there might be money due to her, and if she had money coming, she would let the landlord know where to send it. She would never walk away from money that was owed to her."

"We already tried to get information from the landlord's company and they wouldn't tell us anything," Lauren said.

"I want to try again. Maybe I can talk to someone who's an animal lover. That's how I got the secretary at Sophie's school to tell me Sophie's last name. I asked how she would feel if someone had her dog and didn't know how to get it back to her. Maybe if I tell the landlord that I found Sophie's cat and need to let her family know that Midnight is safe, he would either tell me how to reach her or pass along the message."

"I don't think I saved the name and number," Lauren said,

"but if I found it online once I can find it again. I'll look when I get home."

She called about an hour after I got home and gave me the information I needed. I called the office of Winkowski Associates. I couldn't get through to Mr. Winkowski, but I told his secretary that my friend's family used to rent an apartment from Winkowski Associates and that they had lost their cat when they moved. I laid it on as thick as I could, telling her that Sophie's mother had been sick and that Midnight was Sophie's best friend.

"I found Sophie's cat," I said. "I brought him home with me, but I don't know how to get hold of them to tell them that I have him. I'm trying to get a message to Sophie's family to let them know." I told her Sophie's last name and the address where she had lived.

"I can't give out any information on a former renter," she said, "but I'll see if we have a forwarding address. If we do, I'll write to the family and tell them that you have their cat."

I thanked her, and gave her my contact information. I couldn't think of anything else to do to find Sophie. I hoped Sophie's mother had given the landlord a forwarding address, but did she even know where her family was going when they left? Maybe they were in one of the homeless shelters. Perhaps they were staying temporarily with a friend. They might have gone to Mexico to be with Sophie's grandparents, although that seemed unlikely. Where would they get the money for plane tickets?

Meanwhile, clever Midnight had taken to rubbing on

Mom's ankles and purring. From there, he advanced to jumping into her lap whenever she sat down, and curling into a fur doughnut. Since he also got along well with Waggy, I could tell that Mom wouldn't mind keeping him.

When I told her I wanted to use my allowance to buy a plastic litter pan because the cardboard box had started to stink, she agreed it would be a good idea. She even drove me to the pet store to get one and while we were there she bought more canned cat food, a collar, and a bag of furry toy mice.

On the way home, Mom said, "I'm going to take Midnight to the vet. He needs to be vaccinated and I want to be sure he doesn't have any health problems. We'll make an appointment to have him neutered, too."

"Does this mean Midnight can stay permanently?" I asked.

"It means we'll be Midnight's foster family until you can reach Sophie."

We both knew I might never find Sophie, but if Mom wanted to call Midnight a foster cat, it was okay with me as long as I got to keep him.

As I fell asleep that night with Waggy curled up on one side of me and Midnight snuggled on the other side, I wished Sophie could see us. I wished she could know that Midnight was safe and loved. I hoped she and Trudy were safe and happy, too, but I knew I might never find out what had happened to them.

When I got off the school bus the next afternoon, No Help was waiting for me. He stood half a block away, on the far side of Big Mouth Braider's property, with his arms crossed. He wore jeans and a black hoodie.

I had to walk toward him in order to get home.

If I had seen him before I exited, I would have stayed on the bus and ridden back to school and called Mom for a ride. But I had no reason to survey the sidewalk before I got off the bus so I stepped down as usual, put on my backpack, and heard the bus doors wheeze shut before I looked up.

My mind raced through my options. Turn and run away from him? Go to Mrs. Woodburn's house? What if she wasn't home? Mrs. Braider was the only neighbor who seemed to always be at home, but I couldn't get to her door without going closer to No Help. Should I run all the way to the corner, where Mr. and Mrs. Freeman lived? But the Freemans might not be home, either, and I'd be even farther from my own house.

If I ran, No Help would know I was afraid of him. That would be almost like admitting I was the one who had tipped off the police.

I could pretend I didn't recognize him and walk to my own house, but I knew I couldn't get there before he intercepted me, if that's what he wanted to do.

Acting as if I had not seen him, I pulled out my phone. Mom turned her cell phone off when she was working. Usually I texted her and she responded during her next break. That might be an hour away, or more. I needed to talk to someone now. I scrolled to Lauren's number but before I could place the call, No Help said, "Put the phone away."

He came toward me. I put the phone back in my pocket.

"Why are you here?" I asked.

"I thought I'd look in your front door, the way you looked in mine."

"I don't know what you're talking about."

"I think you do. I saw you staring into my apartment, the day you lied to me about a reward for that cat."

"I didn't lie! I saw posters about a missing cat and it was black, like Sophie's cat. I thought it was hers."

"I searched for those posters but I never found one."

"Maybe someone found the cat and collected the reward, and the posters got taken down."

"And maybe you made the whole thing up to trick me into leaving my apartment so you could go inside and poke around."

"I never went in your apartment. I swear!"

"I suppose you never called the police and told them about me, either."

"Police?" I said, as if I had no idea what he was talking about. "Why would I call the police? I was only trying to find a cat."

He stood directly in front of me now, blocking the sidewalk.

"You're a good liar," he said. "I believed you once, about the reward, but you can't fool me twice. I know you told the cops what you saw in my apartment. Why else would they have come?"

"Am I the only person in the world who ever came to

your door?" I asked. "If someone told the police what you have in your apartment, it was somebody else who went there, because it wasn't me. I don't even know why the police wanted to talk to you."

He shook his head slowly, as if to show he didn't believe me. "No one else I know would rat on me."

"Someone must have."

"Who?"

"How should I know? Somebody you bullied in high school; someone you cut off in traffic; someone who's mad at you. Maybe the man you pushed down the stairs."

"How do you know about that? Who have you been talking to?" His eyes narrowed. "Oh, now I get it," he said. "I thought you were just a punk kid trying to get me in trouble, but now I can see you're working with somebody. Did Max put you up to this?"

"I don't know anyone named Max, and nobody put me up to anything. You have the wrong person. All I did was knock on your door and ask about my friend's cat. That's all! The rest of what you're saying is craziness that doesn't have anything to do with me."

"It makes sense now," he said. "Max plans to cut me out and keep all the money himself. He doesn't have the guts to face me in person so he lets a kid do his dirty work for him." He reached for my arm, but I jerked away.

"Let's go." He motioned for me to go up the walkway toward my house.

"What do you want?" I asked.

"Some friendly conversation. You're going to come with me, and you're going to tell me all about your deal with Max, and then I'll show you what happens to little snoops who poke their noses into other people's business."

"I'm not going anywhere with you," I said. I tried to sprint past him, but he grabbed my arm and twisted it behind my back. He stood directly behind me.

"I have a gun," he said. "Make a sound, and I'll use it."

"You would never get away. My neighbors would hear the shot."

"Maybe they would and maybe they wouldn't. Either way, it would be too late to help you. Now move." He pushed me in front of him toward my house.

"Where are we going?"

"My truck is parked in the alley behind your house. We're going to take a little ride together."

We walked along the side of my house to the backyard. I considered screaming. Mrs. Braider would hear me, but what if she also heard a gunshot? I couldn't take a chance that he really had a gun, and would use it.

Inside the house, Waggy started barking. When I looked at the patio door, I saw him standing on his hind legs, pawing frantically at the glass.

An old white pickup truck was parked behind our garage. I gasped when I saw it. The bed of the truck contained our TV set, Mom and Dad's computer, our stereo system and speakers, and even our microwave oven.

"You broke into my house!" I said.

"Quiet! Get in the truck." He opened the passenger side door and shoved me toward the interior.

As soon as I was in the truck, he slammed the door and ran around the front of the truck to the driver's door. With his attention momentarily off me, I pulled out my phone and selected "create message." I chose Mom's number, and typed "White truck." I started to add "help" but I had only typed the "h" and the "e" when the driver's door jerked open and No Help got in.

I thrust my phone in my pocket so he didn't see it. I knew if he caught me texting he would take the phone away, and it might be my only means of getting help. I kept my hand in my pocket. My finger felt along the phone for the Send button and pushed it, hoping Mom would see the text right away and would figure out what I was trying to tell her.

I thought about Waggy, scratching at the glass, trying to come to my aid. How had No Help kept Waggy from biting him when he was robbing our house? Probably he had bribed Waggy with meat or a dog biscuit. Or maybe he simply said, "Good dog," and friendly old Waggy had licked his hand.

I wondered if No Help had seen Midnight inside my house. If he had, did he recognize Midnight as the cat he had put in the Dumpster? Maybe Waggy's frantic barking and scratching was because he was trying to tell me that someone had hurt Midnight or put him outside.

As we left my neighborhood, No Help kept glancing at the speedometer, and I realized he was staying exactly at the speed limit so he would not get pulled over. His shoulders hunched forward, his face looked tense, and he drummed his fingers nervously on the steering wheel.

I wanted to ask No Help if he had seen my cat but I knew he didn't like cats and I feared it would only make him angry.

I knew Waggy was okay. With any luck, Midnight had recognized the bad person who had thrown him in the Dumpster and had hidden under the bed or in a closet.

Whatever had happened to my pets while No Help robbed us, I knew Mom would soon be home and would take care of them.

But who would take care of me?

CHAPTER FOURTEEN

As Emmy's mother rang up a sale on the cash register in Dunbar's children's department, one of the secretaries from the office approached.

"There's a phone call for you," Mrs. Lopez said. "The woman says it's urgent."

Mrs. Rushford waited while her customer signed the charge slip. She put the receipt in the package and handed it over, saying, "Thank you for shopping at Dunbar's." Then she thanked Mrs. Lopez and hurried toward the phone in the office.

Employees were not supposed to make or receive calls on Dunbar's line, so Mrs. Rushford could not imagine who her caller was. Her friends and family all knew to use her cell phone number, or to leave a message on her home phone.

"Line three," the office manager said, when Mrs. Rushford arrived.

"Hello?" she said. "This is Mrs. Rushford."

"It's Mrs. Braider, from next door."

"Yes?" Mrs. Braider was a busybody who often gossiped to Mrs. Rushford about what went on in the neighborhood, but she had never bothered Mrs. Rushford at work before.

"I'm wondering if you have company," Mrs. Braider said. "Is there supposed to be a man at your house?"

"No. What's going on?"

"When Emmy got off the school bus, a seedy-looking man was waiting for her. He had been standing on the sidewalk by my house for ten minutes. I didn't like the looks of him, so I watched out my front window. The same man was with her one afternoon several days ago."

"Are you sure?"

"Positive. The first time he came he only walked behind her until she went inside, as if he was seeing her safely home. Then he left. This time she talked to him for a while out in front. I couldn't hear what they said, but they appeared to be arguing."

Mrs. Rushford tried to think who the man might be.

Mrs. Braider continued. "He grabbed her arm and twisted it behind her and marched her around the side of your house into the backyard. I don't know what happened after that. You know I don't usually pry into my neighbors' business, but the situation seemed suspicious to me and I thought I should call you."

"You did the right thing. Thank you."

"If you would prune those bushes in your backyard, I

would be able to see better and could tell you what happened after they went around the side of your house."

"Thank you for calling," Mrs. Rushford said. "I'll call Emmy right now to be sure she's okay."

She hung up, took her cell phone out of her pocket, and called Emmy. After ringing four times, the call went to voice mail. "This is Mom," Mrs. Rushford said. "Call me right away."

Who would Emmy have argued with? Why didn't she answer her phone?

She looked at her watch. Not quite four o'clock. She had another hour to go before her shift ended. She was tempted to take an hour of vacation time and leave early, but by the time she got permission to do that and filled out the necessary paperwork, the hour would be nearly up.

She also hesitated because she knew that Mrs. Braider always imagined the worst in every situation and often exaggerated what she saw. She had called the Rushfords' home many times over the years to warn Mr. and Mrs. Rushford of so-called problems. Once she reported that Emmy had been seen buying a ticket for an R-rated movie when Emmy was merely using the Multiplex Theater's common ticket window to buy a ticket for a new Disney film.

Then there was the time Mrs. Braider called at midnight to warn them that Emmy was sneaking out in her pajamas and going who-knows-where with an older man. That night, Emmy had been on her way to a surprise pajama party where the girls who had been selected for the school's drill team were picked up at their homes and taken to the team captain's house. The "older man" had been Lauren's dad, and the Rushfords had known about the plans ahead of time.

In all the years of Mrs. Braider's calls, there had never been a single time when Emmy was actually doing anything wrong.

Still, Mrs. Rushford could hardly believe all the things her daughter had done recently without her knowledge in an attempt to provide food for a needy family and rescue that family's cat. She hoped Emmy was not involved in some other secret scheme to save the world.

She wondered what Mrs. Braider's definition of a "seedy-looking man" might be. Jim Grayson, from the Garden Club, usually wore jeans with holes in the knees and had his shoulder-length hair pulled back in a ponytail. He had stopped by the house last Saturday to return a book he'd borrowed.

For that matter, Mrs. Rushford's younger brother, Josh, who played guitar in a rock band, favored the punk look and had been known to dye his spiked hair purple. He frequently showed up around dinnertime. No doubt Mrs. Braider would consider both Jim Grayson and Josh seedy-looking. However, neither Josh nor Jim Grayson would ever twist Emmy's arm.

Colleen, the part-time clerk, stuck her head in the office door. "Mrs. Murphy wants to know what's keeping you," she said. "She's covering your station but she needs to leave for a meeting."

"Coming," said Mrs. Rushford. Putting her phone in her pocket, she hurried back to the children's department. Once there, though, she kept worrying about Emmy. It was odd that Emmy had not returned her call immediately. Their agreement was that Emmy could have a cell phone if she always had it turned on so that her parents could reach her any time they tried. Until now, Emmy had kept that bargain.

When there was a lull between customers, Mrs. Rushford decided to call again. That's when she saw that a text from Emmy had just arrived. She opened it, and stared at the screen: White truck he

He?

A feeling of dread crept up the back of Mrs. Rushford's neck. She dialed Emmy's number again. It rang and went to voice mail.

"I have to leave," she told Colleen. "Something is wrong at home. I'm afraid Emmy might be in trouble."

She didn't wait for permission from Mrs. Murphy. She didn't bother to punch out on the employee time clock. She didn't even go back to the employee room for her coat. She just grabbed her purse, ran across the parking lot to her car, and headed home.

He. He what? Had Emmy started to identify whoever "he" was? Why had she not finished the text?

Twenty minutes later, Mrs. Rushford drove down the alley and pulled into her garage. She ran to the back door. Although dark clouds hung low overhead, no lights glowed in the house. Waggy barked when she opened the door.

"Emmy?" she called as she turned on the kitchen lights.

Instead of acting all silly as he usually did when someone came home, Waggy whined and panted. He pawed at Mrs. Rushford's pant leg.

"Emmy? Are you here?" Her gaze swept the kitchen. Something seemed different. Something was wrong. She realized that the microwave was gone.

She ran into the family room. The desk top where the computer usually sat was empty. The TV was missing, too.

Trying not to panic, Mrs. Rushford called 911.

"My daughter is missing!" she said. "Someone broke into my house, and Emmy isn't here."

She gave her name and address, as well as Emmy's name and description.

She answered several questions. "The TV is gone, and our computer and our microwave. My neighbor saw Emmy talking to a man who was waiting when she got off the school bus. They argued and the man grabbed her arm and took her into the backyard." Mrs. Rushford started to cry, struggled for control, and continued. "My dog is acting spooked." She stretched one hand down to pat Waggy.

She was told not to touch anything until the police arrived. "Please hurry," she pleaded. "I think Emmy has been abducted."

When she finished the call to the police, she called her husband.

"I'll be on the first flight home," he said.

Mrs. Rushford fervently wished he had been working in his home office this week, rather than in Colorado. It would be hours before he could get home. He might not arrive until the next morning.

She called Mrs. Braider and asked her to come over.

When she explained the situation, Mrs. Braider said, "I knew it! I knew that man was no good the minute I laid eyes on him. I said to myself, I said, Emmy is asking for trouble keeping company with him."

Mrs. Rushford wanted to deny that Emmy was "keeping company" with whoever had been there, but she didn't want to argue with Mrs. Braider. "I'm sure the police will want to question you," she said.

Next she called Lauren and asked if she knew where Emmy was. "She isn't here," Lauren said. "She took the school bus home, like she always does."

By then Mrs. Rushford's hands were shaking so much she could barely hold the phone. She hung up, dropped to her knees, and buried her face in Waggy's fur.

"What happened, Waggy?" she whispered. "Who was in our house?"

CHAPTER FIFTEEN

As I rode through Cedar Hill with No Help, worries bounced around my mind like Ping-Pong balls while I tried to figure out how to save myself.

"White truck" was not a good enough description. I needed to get the license plate number, and text it to Mom. As soon as I got out of the truck, I would look at the license plate and memorize the number.

My phone rang again as No Help drove across town. Although I knew from the news broadcast that his real name was Donald Zummer, I still thought of him as No Help.

I hoped the caller was Mom. If she used her phone, she would see the text I had sent. Of course, the person calling might also be Lauren or Uncle Josh or any one of a dozen other people who often called me.

"Ignore it," he said.

About fifteen minutes later, it rang again.

"Turn the phone off," he said, "and give it to me."

"It'll be my mom. If I don't answer, she'll know something is wrong, and she'll call the police."

"No, she won't. Not yet."

I should have set the phone on vibrate so he didn't hear it ringing. Too late now. Reluctantly, I punched End and handed him my phone, knowing he was right. Mom would worry if I didn't answer or return her call, but she would assume I'd forgotten to turn my phone on when school got out, or had let the battery run down. She wouldn't call the police until she got home and discovered that our house had been burglarized.

I wondered if he really had a gun or if he had been bluffing. I had not seen a gun. If he wasn't armed, I might be able to get away. I could run for it as soon as he stopped the truck. But how did I know for sure? If I took a chance that he had been lying and he actually had a gun, I felt sure he would use it.

Soon I recognized the street we were on. He was taking me to his apartment. If I could get away from him long enough to pound on Mrs. Spangler's door, Mrs. Spangler would let me in. I thought about Mrs. Spangler, moving slowly with her walker. What if she didn't get to the door in time? I didn't know who lived in the other first-floor apartment, but maybe I should go there instead.

The truck passed a young couple pushing a baby stroller. I longed to roll down my window and scream, "Help!" but I feared his reaction. I wished I knew whether he really had a gun.

When we got to Sophie's apartment building, he drove the truck up across the curb, over the grass, and stopped beside the front door.

"You are going to sit right where you are while I unload this stuff," he said. "Don't bother yelling because nobody will hear you. The apartment next to me is empty and the old woman who lives downstairs is deaf as a fence post."

I didn't say anything. I planned to wait until he was partway up the stairs with the TV or the computer console in his arms. Then I would jump out of the truck and run. With him inside the building, I wouldn't be able to go to Mrs. Spangler's apartment or to the other one on the first floor, but I could run between Sophie's building and the next one. I could hide behind the Dumpster, or I could keep running until I flagged down a passing car on the next street over, and got help.

He opened the front door, and propped it open with a rock that was in the back of the truck. Obviously, he had done this before.

He stepped inside and briefly stood by the door to apartment 2, across from Mrs. Spangler. What was he doing? Maybe he was listening to make sure no one was at home who might hear him carrying the goods up the stairs.

He hurried back to the truck, watching me the whole time, and put the tailgate down. When he picked up the microwave, I positioned my hand on the door handle, ready to open it as soon as he got to the top of the stairs.

He carried the microwave inside, glancing back over his shoulder at me every few feet. To my surprise, he did not go up

the stairs. Instead, he turned left and went into apartment 2! I
realized he had not been listening to see if anyone was home in
apartment 2. He had been unlocking the door.

No Help must rent two apartments in this building. I
wondered if the police knew that. Had they searched the
second apartment or was it still full of stolen goods?

He quickly set the microwave inside and returned to the
truck, then carried in the TV and the other items, looking
back at me every few seconds. He was never more than a few
feet from the truck, and he was aware of me the whole time.
If I jumped out of the truck and ran, he would be after me
immediately.

When he finished unloading the truck, he closed the tailgate
and opened the door next to me. "You're next," he said.

As I slid slowly out of the truck, I stared at his pockets,
trying to tell if one of them looked lumpy enough to contain
a handgun. I couldn't be sure. I could tell his pockets weren't
empty, but people carry many items in their pockets: keys,
candy bars, gloves, money. I knew for sure my cell phone was
in one pocket. I wanted to scream for help, but I didn't dare.
What if one of the bulges in his pocket was a gun?

He reached behind the seat of the truck, removed a coil of
white rope, and looped it over his arm. I did not want to think
about how he intended to use it.

As we passed the front of the truck, I read the license
plate number. The number would be important information
to give to the police if I got away. No, I thought. Not if I got
away; when I get away.

A43883J

I repeated it to myself, and made up tricks to help remember it. A is the first letter of the alphabet. Dad is forty-three years old. There are eighty-eight notes on a piano. Three. I couldn't think of anything special for three but J could be for the blue jays that my grandma sees at her bird feeder. I visualized three blue jays.

Mentally I went through the list: A to start the alphabet, Dad's age is forty-three, eighty-eight piano keys, and three blue jays. A-43-88-3J.

We went into the building, and he pointed for me to go up the stairs. In my head I screamed, Mrs. Spangler! Help! Open your door and see what's happening! Call the police!

Mrs. Spangler couldn't hear my thoughts.

He followed me upstairs to the apartment I'd photographed. We went inside. The room contained only a card table and two folding chairs, an air mattress and sleeping bag on the floor, and a couple of empty pizza boxes. A laptop computer sat on the card table.

"Sit here," he said.

I sat on a folding chair.

"Put your hands behind you."

I obeyed.

He wrapped the rope around my wrists, binding them together and then tying them to the chair. Next he tied each of my feet to a chair leg.

"You're going to sit here while I move my truck," he said.

I heard him run down the stairs, heard the truck door

close, heard the engine start. I wiggled my hands, trying to loosen the rope, but I only chafed my wrists.

"Help!" I screamed. "Mrs. Spangler! Help!"

I heard nothing from the apartment below me.

I tried to make the chair slide forward toward the door, thinking if I yelled out the open door Mrs. Spangler might be able to hear me, but the chair didn't move. However, I discovered that I could push with my feet and make the chair slide backward, toward the window. I tried to make the chair slide sideways and turn gradually, so that when I pushed, it would go toward the door. I had turned only a couple of feet when I saw an open pizza box on the floor. There were still two pieces of pizza in it. A small green jackknife lay beside them.

The knife was open. Pizza sauce covered the two-inch long blade, but it looked sharp enough to cut through the rope.

I backed the chair until my hands were above the box. Then I leaned sideways until the chair toppled over. A sharp pain jolted my shoulder when I hit the floor. I waited until it subsided before I moved my hands.

My fingers felt frantically across the box. I touched cardboard. Tomato sauce stuck to my fingertips, but I didn't feel the knife. I tried to make the chair move again by shifting my shoulders, but without having my feet on the floor, I couldn't get any traction.

I heard a faint sound from outside. The truck door slamming shut? The front door closing?

The side of one leg touched the floor. When I pressed that

leg down as hard as I could, the chair slid far enough that my fingertips hit metal.

I strained to pull the knife toward the palm of my hand, but just as I grasped it, I heard his footsteps running back up the stairs, and I knew it was too late. Even if I could somehow pull the blade across the rope without also cutting myself, I didn't have enough time to cut through the rope.

I closed my fingers around the knife's handle, hoping he wouldn't notice that I had it.

He came into the room, stopped, and stared at me. He closed the door behind him, and then walked over to where I lay helplessly on my side, still tied to the chair. He put both hands on my shoulders and lifted my chair until it was upright again. I gritted my teeth from pain when his hand gripped the shoulder that had landed on the floor, but I managed not to cry out. I didn't want him to know I'd been injured.

He frowned at the empty box. Then he looked behind me at my hands, and his expression changed as he saw the knife and realized what I had done. He slowly shook his head.

"That was a bad idea," he said as he pried open my fingers and took the knife away from me. He wiped the blade on his pant leg to remove any traces of pizza, folded up the knife, and put it in his pants pocket.

He sat backward on the other chair with his hands crossed on the chair back, leaning toward me. "Okay," he said. "Tell me about your deal with Max."

"I told you, I don't know anyone named Max," I said. "There is no deal."

"Then why did the cops come poking around here with a search warrant?"

"How would I know? The only times I came here were to bring food to Sophie and to look for her cat. After she moved, I had no reason to return."

He appeared to be thinking about what I'd said.

"Maybe you should be asking Max your questions, instead of asking me," I said. "It sounds to me as if you've been double-crossed."

"I think you're lying. It's too much of a coincidence that I catch you looking in my apartment and then the cops show up, asking questions."

"When did the cops come?" I asked.

"Wednesday."

"I haven't been here since last week. If I had seen something suspicious and gone to the police, don't you think they would have investigated sooner?"

He did not reply.

"So is Max the only other person who's seen your apartment?" I asked. "No other visitors?"

He slapped his hand on the card table, making me jump. "Gunther!" he exclaimed. "The last time Max was here, his kid brother, Gunther, was with him. He asked a bunch of questions about how much things were worth, and I got mad and told him to wait for his brother outside."

No Help stood and began pacing around the room. "Gunther turned me in," he said. "That little toad! He probably thinks he'll become Max's new partner. Oh, he is going to be sorry he did that. He is going to be very, very sorry!"

For a second I thought, Poor Gunther. I've sicced No Help on him and he won't know why. Then I remembered that Gunther knew about Max and No Help's burglaries and had apparently done nothing to stop them.

"Now that you know it wasn't me," I said, "can you please untie me and let me leave? My mother will be home from work by now and she'll be worried."

He stopped pacing and looked at me as if he had never seen me before. "You," he said. "What am I going to do about you?"

"You don't have to do anything about me. You don't even need to drive me home; I know where to catch the bus."

"I can't let you go home. You'll call the cops the second you're out of here."

"No, I won't. You have my phone."

"There are people with cell phones everywhere." He began pacing again. "I might get off with community service and a fine on the burglary charge but not for this. Not for taking a kid."

"I won't tell anyone about you."

"And I'm the next president of the United States."

"The longer you keep me, the worse it will be when they catch you," I said.

"They aren't going to catch me. It's time for me to get out of this dump."

He looked out the window and spoke as if he were talking to himself. "I'll pawn everything, keep all the money, and hit the road. By the time Max realizes I'm gone, I'll be in another state."

He unplugged the laptop and closed it. He glanced around the room and then started for the door.

"What about me?" I asked.

"You're staying here."

"You can't leave me here," I said.

"Max will find you when he comes looking for me."

I wondered how long that would be. Days? Weeks?

"I could starve to death before I'm found. Then you'd be wanted for murder."

"It doesn't matter what I'm wanted for because they won't find me."

CHAPTER SIXTEEN

I needed to stall him. I had to keep him here until I figured out a way to get help.

"I have to use the bathroom," I said.

He shook his head. "Too bad. I don't have time for that."

"What's your hurry?"

"I have to load the stuff that's downstairs, plus I have another full room in a building down the street."

"I thought the police took all the things you stole."

"Only from this apartment." A smug smile crept across his face. "The cops didn't find out about the downstairs apartment or the place Max rents."

He put his hand on the doorknob.

"I have to go really bad!"

"Not my problem," he said.

"You could untie me and lock me in the room. I can use

the bathroom while you go get your truck. Then you can tie me up again. It won't take more than a minute or two."

"Forget it. I'm out of here." He opened the door and stepped into the hall.

Mentally I scrambled to think of a way to talk him into untying me. Money, I thought. What he cares about is money.

"Your landlord won't give you back the damage deposit on this apartment if I pee all over the floor," I said. "Mr. Winkowski is really fussy about the damage deposit."

He turned back, stepping into the room again. "How do you know who the landlord is?"

"Sophie told me. She said they didn't get their deposit back because Mr. Winkowski found out they'd had a cat inside when pets aren't allowed."

He walked over to where I sat and glared down at me.

"Even though Midnight didn't do any damage," I added, "Mr. Winkowski wouldn't refund their money, so you know he won't give you anything if the room smells like urine. How much was the deposit? Two hundred dollars? Three hundred?"

He swore under his breath, but he put the laptop on the floor, jerked on the rope ends to untie the knots, and began to unbind my feet and hands.

I could hardly believe my argument about a damage deposit had worked. Didn't he realize that in order to get the deposit he would have to tell his landlord where to send the refund check, which meant the police would be able to find him, too?

He pulled the rope loose. I stood, shaking my hands to get the circulation back.

"Make it fast," he said.

After insisting I needed a bathroom, I really did have to go so I hurried into the bathroom, closed the door, and turned the lock. One look at the toilet and sink convinced me he would never get any damage deposit back no matter what I did.

"Hurry up!" he yelled.

I didn't have time to clean the fixtures. I used the toilet, promising myself I'd take a shower the minute I got out of there. While the toilet flushed I put the plug in the bathtub drain and turned on both the faucets. I did the same in the sink. I hoped that the noise of the toilet flushing would cover up the sound of running water.

The old fixtures had no emergency overflow drains. It shouldn't take long for the water to run over the tops of the sink and tub. Then water would soak through the floor, and Mrs. Spangler's ceiling would drip. She would call the landlord. Winkowski Associates would send a plumber out, and the plumber would find me. I hoped the water wouldn't do too much damage to Mrs. Spangler's apartment.

"Come on!" he yelled.

I slipped out of the bathroom, closing the door firmly behind me. No Help stood beside the chair, holding the rope.

"Sit!" he commanded.

I sat.

I kept talking, hoping my voice would prevent him from hearing the running water. Instead of begging him to let me go, I asked him where he had met Max.

"He used to work with me, when I washed dishes at

Porky's Pig Palace. He helped in the kitchen. I could barely make my truck payments but he always had money to burn, so I asked him how he managed it. He told me he ran his own business on the side."

He grabbed my hands, bound them the same way he had before, then tied my ankles. He was rougher this time, jerking on the rope in his hurry to leave.

"What kind of business?"

"That's what I wanted to know. I kept pestering him with more questions until he asked if I would be interested in helping him. Two weeks later we both quit Porky's. We've been partners ever since. Until now."

As soon as I was tied to the chair again, he picked up the laptop and headed for the door.

Hurry, I thought. *Get out of here.* I wanted him gone before any water came under the bathroom door.

No Help turned the catch so that the door would lock behind him. Then he stepped into the hallway and pulled the door shut. I heard his feet clatter down the stairs.

When No Help left, any danger of my getting shot went with him. I still had more problems than a stray cat has fleas, but at least an angry thief with a gun was no longer one of them.

If he planned to pawn the items that were stored downstairs, plus a room full of stolen goods that were stashed somewhere down the street, it would take him a while to get it all loaded onto the truck. Maybe Mrs. Spangler or someone else would notice what he was doing and wonder about it.

Or maybe not. Mrs. Spangler hadn't opened her door when he was unloading the truck earlier. She probably wouldn't look out now. Maybe she didn't hear him.

If someone walked past on the sidewalk or drove down the street while No Help loaded his truck, they'd assume he was moving. There would be no reason to call the police.

Outside, daylight gave way to darkness. Inside, the walls seemed to slide closer as it became harder to see, until I could only make out an oblong of gray where the window was. Soon that, too, turned black.

I wished he had turned on the light. Even the bare bulb beside a dangling ceiling chain would be better than waiting in the dark. I took a deep breath, telling myself to stay calm.

I did not feel calm; I felt panicky. I was alone in an empty apartment miles from where I lived. I was tied up and abandoned, and nobody knew where I was.

I wondered how long it would take for the water to overflow the tub and sink, and start under the bathroom door.

A tear rolled down one cheek. I couldn't brush it away because my hands were tied, so I gritted my teeth and forced myself not to cry. I refused to start bawling and get myself all stuffed up when I couldn't even blow my nose.

My shoulder throbbed where it had hit the floor when I tipped the chair over. I sat in the darkness, listening. Faint noises from Mrs. Spangler's TV drifted upward. Twice, headlights briefly illuminated the window as a car drove past.

I shivered. Was there any heat in this apartment? Probably not. I realized my feet were cold because my sneakers were wet. I couldn't lean over to feel how deep the water was but I could lift my toes a couple of inches. I raised them as far as I could and then stomped down. Splash! Water flew up, splattering both legs of my jeans. There must already be an inch or more on the floor. Soon I felt it seep over the tops of my sneakers.

I had assumed the water would soak through the floor and cause a leak to the room below, or that it would run under the door to the hallway and cascade down the stairs. Either way, the water would alert Mrs. Spangler, or anyone else who saw it, that there was plumbing trouble in No Help's apartment. I had not expected the water to stay in his apartment, getting deeper and deeper while I sat tied to a chair, unable to get away.

I remembered that the stairway was permanently lit, but when I squinted at the bottom of the door I couldn't see even a sliver of light. The door fit so tightly that there wasn't space for the water to escape.

I learned to swim when I was only three, and every summer Lauren and I spend hot afternoons at the public pool. My family enjoys going to the beach, too.

This was different. When I'm in the pool, I can swim to the side and hoist myself up any time I want to, or go to the shallow end and walk up the steps to the pool deck. At the ocean, I always run along the edge, letting the waves lap over my bare feet, squishing the wet sand between my toes.

I had never before been in danger from water. If this water didn't soak through the floor or flow under the door to the hall, it would keep rising until someone turned off the faucets and pulled the plugs out of the drains. It would come up and up, past my knees, my waist, and my shoulders while I sat helpless, unable to make it stop.

CHAPTER SEVENTEEN

Three police cars stopped in front of the Rushford residence. Mrs. Rushford, who had been watching from the window, flung open the door as the officers hurried toward her. Two officers from one car headed toward the back of the Rushfords' house, one on each side. Two other officers went to the door.

"I'm Sergeant Whitman," the tall gray-haired officer said. "This is Lieutenant Benson."

Mrs. Rushford introduced herself and Mrs. Braider.

"Tell us what happened," Sergeant Whitman said.

Mrs. Rushford went through the whole story. Mrs. Braider told what she had witnessed. "Emmy is not answering her phone," Mrs. Rushford said. "She always either answers or calls back within a minute or two. Always! Something is wrong." Her voice broke. "Something is terribly wrong."

"I believe we can issue an AMBER Alert," Sergeant

Whitman said. "We'll need a current picture of Emmy."

Mrs. Rushford had seen AMBER Alerts in the past, where the description and photo of a missing child were sent to local radio and TV stations who interrupt their programming to broadcast the information. The child's name and description are also displayed in bright lights over all the major freeways, along with any information about the suspected abductor and his/her vehicle. More than once, a citizen who had seen an AMBER Alert recognized the missing child or a suspect's vehicle and alerted authorities.

"I carry her most recent school picture in my wallet," Mrs. Rushford said.

One of the officers who had gone to the backyard now came inside and got permission to search the bedrooms and the rest of the house. Meanwhile, Mrs. Rushford opened her purse, removed the wallet, and found Emmy's picture. She slipped it out of the protective sleeve and handed it to Sergeant Whitman.

He looked at the photo. "A lovely girl," he said. "We'll do our best to find her."

"Thank you," Mrs. Rushford said, once again choking back tears.

Sergeant Whitman handed the picture to Lieutenant Benson, who looked at it and gasped.

"I met this girl," she said. "I didn't recognize the name, but I know the face. She came into the station and turned over photos that she took of an apartment full of stolen goods."

Mrs. Rushford's hand flew to her throat. "What?" she said. "When was this?"

"Only a few days ago. Her tip led to the arrest of a man who had burglarized nearly two dozen homes. She showed me the photos and gave me his address."

"Is that the one who got caught red-handed with his apartment full of stolen computers and TVs?" Sergeant Whitman asked. "I wasn't involved in the case, but I heard about it."

"That's the one. Donald Zummer. He was arraigned yesterday."

"Are you sure it was Emmy?" Mrs. Rushford asked. She found it hard to believe that only a short time after confessing all of her trips to Sophie's neighborhood and promising never to do anything like that again, Emmy would not only get involved with a burglary suspect, but also would go to the police with photos and not tell her parents what she had done.

"It was her," Lieutenant Benson said. "I have the paperwork on file that she filled out when she showed me the pictures. I remember now, she said her name was Louise."

"That's her middle name," Mrs. Rushford said. "She's named after my mother, Emmy Louise."

"I recommended that she tell her parents about the photos," Lieutenant Benson said. "Obviously that didn't happen."

"No," Mrs. Rushford said. "It didn't."

"Where's the burglary suspect now?" Sergeant Whitman asked. "Is Zummer still locked up?"

Lieutenant Benson shook her head. "It was a first offense," she said. "The judge let him go when his business partner posted twenty-thousand-dollars' bail."

The two officers looked at each other. "I don't like this," Lieutenant Benson said.

"So if he posted bail, he could leave," said Mrs. Rushford. "He was free to go. Is that right?"

"Correct," said Sergeant Whitman.

Mrs. Braider said, "He might have figured out who tipped off the cops and come after her."

This time, Mrs. Rushford did not even try to hold back her tears.

"Emmy believed that the suspect did not know she had taken the pictures," Lieutenant Benson said.

Using a handheld computer, Lieutenant Benson found the photo of Mr. Zummer that was taken the day of his arrest. She inserted it in a file of generic mug shots and then said, "Mrs. Braider, I'd like you to look at a few photos, and tell me if you recognize any of them." She began scrolling through the pictures while Mrs. Braider concentrated on the screen. When Donald Zummer's picture appeared, Mrs. Braider cried, "That's him! That's the man who was with Emmy."

"You're sure?"

"I'm positive. He came here once before, and he's the one who pushed Emmy into the backyard this afternoon."

As soon as the rest of the house had been checked, all the police officers left.

"We'll be in touch," Sergeant Whitman said.

Mrs. Rushford wiped away her tears as she thanked them.

Before driving away, Sergeant Whitman sent in all the information needed for the AMBER Alert, which went into effect immediately. Using a portable scanner, he e-mailed Emmy's photo. Within minutes, her picture and the police department's mug shot of the suspect were sent to media contacts, the State Patrol, and the National Crime Information Center. Thousands of cell-phone users who had registered for the Wireless AMBER Alert program were notified.

Meanwhile, Lieutenant Benson checked the Department of Motor Vehicles to find out if a vehicle was registered to Donald Zummer. She quickly had her answer. Mr. Zummer owned a 1972 Ford truck. License number A43883J. Color: white.

Lieutenant Benson called the police dispatcher and added a description of the truck to the AMBER Alert. She also asked the dispatcher for the address of Zummer's apartment. She remembered where it was but needed the exact street number in order to call for backup.

With any luck, he would be there, and Emmy Louise Rushford would be with him. Unharmed.

She called for backup as she drove, explaining the connection between her destination and the child who had triggered the AMBER Alert. As she turned onto East Sycamore, two other squad cars converged. The three officers jumped from their cars and sprinted toward the front of the building.

They were almost to the door when they got an All-Points Bulletin. "A truck matching the one in the AMBER Alert has been spotted going North on Highway 405, just past the Coal Creek exit in Bellevue. All available units respond."

The three officers ran back to their squad cars and took off in pursuit of the truck.

CHAPTER EIGHTEEN

The water climbed slowly toward my knees. Although I had turned on both the hot and cold faucets, there was no warmth in the dampness that soaked my jeans. All the hot water must have been used up.

I inhaled, trying to settle my nerves, but the air smelled acrid, as if the water was contaminated. I remembered the filthy sink, toilet, and bathtub, and the dust balls, hair, and dirt on the bathroom floor. The apartment had probably not been cleaned since No Help rented it. No wonder the water smelled yucky.

My eyes had adjusted to the dark. I saw a pizza box floating near my chair like a square brown raft.

I shivered. My panic rose as fast as the murky water.

If I get out of this mess, I told myself, I will never, ever do anything remotely dangerous again. I should have shown the photos to Mom and Dad and let them be the ones to contact the police. At the very least, I should have let them know what I had done, even if it meant losing privileges. I would rather be grounded for the rest of the year than drown in No Help's apartment.

A sudden shriek of sirens in the distance made my heart flutter. My hopes soared as the sounds came closer. The sirens stopped nearby and blue lights arced in circles outside the window, as if the police cars had parked in front of Sophie's building and left their lights moving.

"Yes!" I shouted. "I'm up here! Hurry!"

I listened for voices. I anticipated someone knocking on the door, but it didn't happen. Instead, after only a minute or so I saw the blue lights leave. The sirens screamed again but this time they went away from me, fading into the distance until the shrill sounds dimmed and disappeared.

I closed my eyes and let my head droop down as my optimism fled with the police cars.

Mrs. Spangler also heard the sirens and noticed the blue lights outside. She went to the window and looked out. Three police cars were parked directly in front of her building. She watched as three officers started toward the front door, stopped, then turned and rushed back to their cars and drove off.

Gracious! What was that all about? It was more exciting outside her window than it was on the TV. She turned the program off and slowly made her way to her bedroom where she put on her favorite flannel nightgown, the blue and white one her daughter had sent for her birthday. The next time Marcia called, she would tell her about the police cars. She liked to have something interesting to tell her daughter. Marcia always liked it when Mrs. Spangler had tidbits of news to relate.

Mrs. Spangler brushed her teeth and eased her weary bones into bed. She wished she could still care for a pet. After Richard died, it had been comforting to curl up with Penny, the Pomeranian that she and Richard had rescued from the shelter all those years ago. The warmth of the small dog beside her had made the bed less lonely, and she had liked the soft snuffling noises that Penny used to make in her sleep. When Penny died at the age of nineteen, Mrs. Spangler had thought her heart would break.

Sighing, she closed her eyes. There was no use weeping for times past. I am lucky, she told herself, to have such happy memories. She let her thoughts drift back to when Penny's predecessor, Muffin, was a young dog and Richard was healthy and Marcia still lived at home. What good times those had been!

She smiled, and snuggled under the quilt.

Plop!

Mrs. Spangler's eyes flew open. What was that?

Plop! Plop! It sounded like water dripping. She must not have shut the faucet off all the way. She sat up, fumbled for her glasses, and turned on the light. She swung her feet to the floor and reached for her walker.

Plop! There it was again. She pushed her walker into the bathroom, but the faucets were not dripping. Mrs. Spangler frowned. Could it be the kitchen faucet? She stood still, listening.

Plop! Plop! She started down the hall. Plop! What on earth? It seemed to be coming from the living room. It couldn't be a leaky roof, not when she lived in a first-floor apartment. Besides, it wasn't raining tonight.

She made her way into the living room, turning on lights as she went. The plopping sounds came faster, and she followed them until she found a large puddle on the floor beside the sofa. Looking up, she saw a dark stain on the ceiling. Water dripped from it to the floor below.

Mrs. Spangler inched her walker to the kitchen, took her largest pan out of the cupboard, and put the pan where it would catch the drips.

That awful man upstairs must have let his bathtub overflow. Or maybe his toilet had stuck and he didn't know it. Probably he wasn't at home. He didn't seem to spend much time here.

She didn't know his name, so she couldn't call him. She knew from past experience that there was no use trying to call her landlord except during business hours because all she got was an answering machine. Well, she couldn't wait until tomorrow morning to notify someone. By then, the whole ceiling might fall in.

Mrs. Spangler called 911. "There's water coming through my ceiling from the apartment above me," she said.

"Have you called the person who lives there?"

"I don't have his number. I don't even know his name."

"Can you go upstairs to talk to him?"

"I'm eighty-nine years old and I use a walker. I can't go up the stairs."

"Did you call the apartment manager, or the landlord?"

"There is no manager. The landlord only takes calls between eight and five."

"What's the address?"

"1135 East Sycamore. Apartment one."

"I'll send someone to help you, ma'am." The 911 operator knew most of the police were attempting to stop the fleeing truck from the AMBER Alert. If no officer was available, he would ask a firefighter to check on Mrs. Spangler.

Mrs. Spangler thanked the operator. She put on her yellow bathrobe and her fuzzy slippers while she waited for help to arrive.

The police dispatcher frowned at the address the 911 operator gave him. It seemed familiar. Had something else happened there recently? He scrolled back through the calls he'd taken earlier that evening. When he got to the request for Donald Zummer's address, he stopped.

How odd. It seemed unlikely that an elderly woman would have a water problem on the same night that someone else in her building was accused of abducting a child. The hairs on the back of his neck prickled. He had learned long ago to trust his intuition about 911 callers and emergency situations. Instead of asking a firefighter to check out the problem, he called Lieutenant Benson.

"Benson here."

"Have you been to that apartment on East Sycamore yet?"

"I got there but didn't go in because I heard the alert that Zummer's truck had been spotted. I'm on my way to 405."

The dispatcher told Lieutenant Benson about Mrs. Spangler's call. "It seemed too much of a coincidence," he said, "so I thought I'd run it past you before I call the fire station."

"There are plenty of other units following that truck," Lieutenant Benson said. "I'll head back to East Sycamore."

Mrs. Spangler stood in the open doorway of her apartment, waiting. When Lieutenant Benson opened the front door, Mrs. Spangler said, "Look!"

A thin stream of water now trickled down the stairs.

Lieutenant Benson took the stairs two at a time. When she reached the top, she saw water oozing under the door to apartment 4, the same apartment she had entered with a search warrant when she arrested Donald Zummer.

CHAPTER NINETEEN

I heard the sirens approach again but after what had happened earlier, I didn't assume that the police cars were coming to rescue me.

Once again they seemed to stop in front of Sophie's building. When I saw the whirling blue light outside the window, I dared to hope they were headed here.

The water covered my knees and soaked the seat of the chair. I trembled both from the cold and from fear.

I heard footsteps thump up the stairs.

"Help!" I yelled.

Someone pounded on the door. "Police! Open up!"

"I'm tied up! I can't open the door!"

I heard a thud, as if something hard had rammed into the door. A second thud followed. This time I heard wood splintering and then a loud BANG as the door fell forward onto the floor. Water splashed over me when the door landed.

"Emmy Rushford?" the officer said. "Is that you?"

"Yes! I'm here!" I felt as if it were my birthday and the Fourth of July and the first day of summer vacation all rolled into one.

The officer shined a flashlight around the room. The beam of light swept across my chest, glinted off the water, and illuminated the officer's face.

I recognized Lieutenant Benson, the one who had downloaded my photos. "Are you injured?" she asked.

My teeth chattered so hard I could hardly talk. "I'm not hurt, just cold. The water's coming from the bathroom."

Lieutenant Benson turned off the faucets and removed the drain plugs before she started to untie me. By then the water level had already dropped several inches as the water flowed out the open door and down the stairs.

"I am really glad to see you," I said as she undid the knots in the rope. What an understatement! Five minutes earlier every muscle in my body had been tense with fear. Now that tension had dissolved, replaced by relief and gratitude.

"I'm glad to see you, too," she said. "Your mother is frantic."

As soon as I was free, Lieutenant Benson called headquarters. "Emmy Rushford is safe," she said. "Request paramedics at 1135 East Sycamore to check her condition. She appears unharmed."

When the call ended she said, "Your parents are being notified." Then she added, "It's odd. Your mother seems to think your name is Emmy, not Louise."

"I didn't use my first name when I gave you the photos," I said, "because I didn't want the thief to find out it was me who turned the photos in."

"So much for that plan."

"How did you know where to find me?"

"The woman who lives below this apartment called 911 because water was dripping through her ceiling."

I grinned. "Then one of my plans worked," I said.

"You're the one who turned on the faucets and plugged the drains?"

I nodded. "It was the only way I could think of to call attention to the fact that I was here."

A Medic One van arrived. The two medics quickly wrapped a blanket around me, and then took my temperature and blood pressure. They examined my wrists where the rope had been.

While I was being checked, more police officers arrived.

"Why are they here?" I asked.

Lieutenant Benson said, "Kidnap is considered a priority felony case. This apartment is a crime scene and needs to be secured."

The medics decided I did not need to be transported to the hospital.

"I just want to go home," I said.

"That's where we're going," Lieutenant Benson said.

I followed Lieutenant Benson down the stairs. Mrs. Spangler stood in her open doorway, watching all the activity. She had laid a folded blanket across her threshold, to keep the water out of her apartment.

"Emmy!" she said, when she saw me. "What in the world are you doing here? What's going on?"

"Your neighbor abducted me! He tied me up and left me in his apartment."

"Why would he do that?" Mrs. Spangler asked. "Are you all right? Did he hurt you?"

"No. I'm okay." I had finally stopped shivering.

"Where's all the water coming from?"

"The water has been turned off," Lieutenant Benson said, "and your landlord will get an emergency call right away. Is there a bulge in your ceiling or is it just dripping?"

"It's dripping."

"Someone from the city building department will be here within an hour," Lieutenant Benson said, "to decide if it's safe for you to stay."

"She can come to my house," I said.

Lieutenant Benson said, "Do you want to stay here until your ceiling gets checked, or come with us?"

"I'll stay," Mrs. Spangler said, "but thank you for the offer."

Lieutenant Benson ushered me to the squad car and offered me a dry blanket in exchange for the first one, which was now damp. I buckled my seat belt, then draped the blanket over myself. I wasn't cold any more but I couldn't stop shaking. I felt anxious again, as if I expected another catastrophe to occur at any moment.

Watching all the police activity had reminded me that, even though I was now going home, No Help had not yet been captured. He would learn of my rescue. Then what?

If he managed to escape, would he harbor a grudge? Would he return some time in the future, still blaming me for his problems?

Reporters from the TV stations and the local newspaper milled around our front yard. A van that said KOMO on the side was double-parked in front of Mrs. Braider's house. Bright lights illuminated the crowd. They couldn't have arrived so soon after I was found; they must have come because of the AMBER Alert.

As Lieutenant Benson and I got out of the car, the lights focused on us. Cameras whirred and flashed.

Mom had been watching for us and she came flying through the crowd, hugging me and weeping. I shed happy tears myself. Even Mrs. Braider cried.

Lieutenant Benson steered me through the media people, who thrust microphones in our direction while they shouted questions.

"We'll have a statement in about half an hour," Lieutenant Benson told them, but they kept calling to us anyway.

We trooped inside, where Waggy pranced around like a circus pony, acting as if he had not seen me for a year.

"I called your dad to tell him you're safe and that he doesn't need to come home," Mom said, "but he's coming anyway. He booked a midnight flight. He said he needs to see you for himself."

I quickly changed into dry clothes, and then we all gathered in the living room. Sergeant Whitman had arrived, and was talking to Lieutenant Benson.

I had never seen Mrs. Braider smile so much. A truly newsworthy disaster had finally occurred, and she had been an important witness.

It took a while for me to tell them everything that had happened. While I talked, Sergeant Whitman kept glancing at his computer. In the middle of my report, he said, "You might want to turn on the TV. They've caught our suspect."

When the TV came on, big letters filled the screen: BREAKING NEWS. I was startled to see my picture appear. A reporter said, "Emmy Rushford, the twelve-year-old girl who was abducted earlier this evening, is safe. She was found tied to a chair in an empty apartment on East Sycamore Street in Cedar Hill. The AMBER Alert has been canceled."

The scene changed to an aerial shot, taken from a helicopter. I could see the white truck, its bed piled high with stolen items, pulled to the side of the freeway. Police cars surrounded it, lights flashing.

"The suspect in this case has been apprehended," the reporter said. "Thanks to the AMBER Alert, a citizen recognized the suspect's truck, called 911, and told police the truck's location. After a high-speed chase down Interstate 405, police used spike strips to stop the suspect's vehicle. As officers approached, he fired a gun out the window of the truck, but did not hit anyone. When he realized he was surrounded by police, he dropped his weapon and surrendered."

So he did have a gun, I thought. It's a good thing I didn't try to run from him.

No Help stood next to the truck while the officers

handcuffed him. As I watched him being put into a squad car, the anxiety seeped out of me.

"No doubt he'll plead not guilty to abducting Emmy," Sergeant Whitman said.

"I got the license plate number of the truck that he put me in," I said. I thought for a minute. The start of the alphabet, Dad's age, piano keys, and three blue jays at Grandma's bird feeder. I said, "A-43-88-3J."

The corners of Sergeant Whitman's mouth curved into a smile. "He won't be able to deny that he's the one who took you," he said.

"There won't be any bail offered this time," Lieutenant Benson said. "Mr. Zummer is going to prison."

I felt completely safe for the first time since the day he had ridden home with me on the bus.

The news story ended with a promise to update the viewers as soon as more information was available. Mom turned off the television.

I told Lieutenant Benson that No Help had another apartment where he kept stolen goods. "He also has a partner named Max who used to work with him in the kitchen of Porky's Pig Palace," I said. "Max rents an apartment a few doors down from Sophie's building. He kept stolen goods there, too. No Help, I mean Mr. Zummer, said the police had not found it."

"You do good work," Lieutenant Benson said. "We may have to put you on the force."

"Emmy is done tracking down criminals," Mom said.

"That's for sure," I said.

Lieutenant Benson said she needed to give a statement to the press and asked Mom if she wanted to say anything. Mom stood in front of the microphone and said, "I am grateful to the police for bringing Emmy home safely. Thank you to everyone who paid attention to the AMBER Alert and watched for the suspect's truck."

When the officers and Mrs. Braider left, I searched for Midnight but I didn't find him. Mom and I turned the TV on again. This time my jaw dropped as I heard Lieutenant Benson declare I was a hero! "By turning on the faucets, Emmy made sure that she would be found. She had also memorized the license plate number of the suspect's truck, so he can't deny that he abducted her."

As I listened to the broadcast, Midnight crept into the room, swishing his tail nervously. "Where were you?" I cried as I scooped him up and hugged him. "I was afraid something had happened to you."

Midnight refused to be petted. Instead, he struggled to get down and headed for his food bowl.

Mom checked my sore shoulder, which now had a purple bruise, and gave me some ibuprofen.

Dad got home in the middle of the night so I didn't get a whole lot of sleep but I went to school the next day, anyway. Mom and Dad drove me.

When I got to my classroom, Shoeless high-fived me and Jelly Bean pounded his crutches on the floor. My classmates crowded around, telling me they had seen my picture on TV.

They asked a zillion questions and Mrs. Reed let me answer all of them, even after the bell rang.

Crystal's eyes grew wide as she listened. When I told about leaving Sycamore Street, she gasped. "You rode in a cop car?" she asked. She said it as if I had ridden home on the back of a vicious grizzly bear.

"Lieutenant Benson drove me home."

"You should never ride in a cop car," Crystal declared.

Shoeless interrupted. "It will make your teeth turn black," he said. "Right, Crystal?" He almost fell out of his chair laughing at his own wit. The other kids laughed, too.

"Class!" Mrs. Reed said. "Quiet, please. We want to hear about Emmy's experience."

Before I could continue, Crystal blurted, "Riding in cop cars causes . . ."

Mrs. Reed said, "Crystal! Stop. It is Emmy's turn to talk." She nodded at me, and I finished telling them what had happened.

A few days after my rescue, Dunbar's announced that a sixty-eight-year-old woman who said she wanted a clothes dryer had won Dunbar's Dream Contest. The woman had hung her laundry outside to dry her whole life, but now she had back problems, and it was getting too hard for her to carry the heavy loads of wash.

"As soon as I read her entry," Mom said, "I hoped she would be the winner. It's nice to know that all the time I spend reading entries results in something good happening to someone who deserves it."

I thought about Sophie, who had received food as a result of entering the contest even though she was not an official winner. Thinking of Sophie was like reading an exciting mystery novel that's missing the last chapter. I had lots of questions, but no answers. I wondered where she lived now. I hoped she and Trudy were safe, and had enough to eat.

The next afternoon, Mrs. Reed asked me to stay behind when the class went outside for recess. As my classmates filed out the door, Mrs. Reed handed me an envelope.

"This letter is for you," she said, "but it was sent to my attention."

Crystal said, "Emmy's going to be on *The Today Show*. That letter probably explains that she has to wear something green. Otherwise the cameras make your nose appear too big."

Several kids stopped walking and gawked until Mrs. Reed said, "Emmy is not going to be on *The Today Show*."

I looked at the return address on the envelope. Sophie Stanford. Stanford? Had Sophie changed her last name? Or had she been registered at school under a false name? The street address was in Liberty, Missouri.

Missouri! How did Sophie get all the way to Missouri? Instead of following my classmates outside, I sat at my desk and opened the envelope.

Dear Emmy,
*   I hope you get this letter. I remembered your teacher's name from when I saw you at the hospital. I thought it*

*was better to contact you through her than to try to send
another letter to Dunbar's.*

*I am in Missouri, living with Mama's cousin, Joanie.
She and her husband, Doug, paid for our plane tickets
after Mama called Joanie and told her that we had to
move out of our apartment because Mama had been too
sick to work, and we didn't have money to pay the rent.*

*The best news is that we no longer have to hide. The
reason I couldn't let Mrs. Reed help us, and why Mama
would never ask for help from the food bank or any other
agency, was because my uncle, my father's brother, was
searching for us.*

*Two years ago, my father got a sickness called E. coli
from eating tainted chicken. When he died, his brother
accused Mama of poisoning him! This was not true, but my
uncle, who drank too much and didn't think clearly, vowed
revenge. Mama took Trudy and me away and used a different
last name. We had been hiding from him ever since.*

*When Mama got out of the hospital, we returned
to our apartment, but we could not stay there any longer
without paying the rent we owed. We had no place to go.
We slept in a shelter for homeless people for a few nights,
until a social worker there talked Mama into calling
Cousin Joanie. That's when Mama learned that my uncle
went to Alcoholics Anonymous a year ago, quit drinking,
and admits that his brother was not poisoned.*

We are no longer afraid!

*Mama is well now and tomorrow she starts her new
job in the cafeteria of the school where Joanie teaches. I
am in the fifth grade at the same school. I like my teacher
because she reads to us every day.*

*That is all the good news. The bad news is that
Midnight escaped the day the ambulance came, and I never
found him. Even though I called and called him the day
we moved out, he did not come. It broke my heart to leave
him behind. Joanie and Doug have two cats, but I still miss
Midnight and worry about him.*

*You have already done so much to help me that I hate
to ask another favor of you, but if you could go to my old
apartment and look for Midnight I would be so grateful. I
don't want him to be cold and hungry.*

*Thank you again for helping my family. We will stay
in Missouri now, so I probably won't see you again. Cousin
Joanie's address is on the envelope. If you find Midnight,
please let me know.*

Your friend,
Sophie

Clearly, Sophie had not heard from Winkowski Associates
that I had Midnight. Maybe Sophie's mom hadn't sent them
the Missouri address. Any damage deposit may have been kept
for rent owed.

When I showed Sophie's letter to my parents, Dad said,
"We can send Midnight to her. He can go on a plane."

"He would be scared out of his mind if he was alone in

a cat carrier on an airplane," I said. "He'd have to ride in the baggage section."

"Yes," Dad admitted, "he probably would be frightened. But he is Sophie's cat, and I don't know any other way to get him to her."

I stared at my shoes. "I wouldn't have to tell her that I have him," I said.

They waited until I looked up at them.

"Sophie is worried about him," Mom said. "You need to let her know that he is safe."

Dad added, "How would you feel if Waggy was lost and you never knew what happened to him?"

I had used that same argument on the secretary at Sophie's school.

If Waggy was lost, I would be devastated. I knew I would want the person who found him to return him, even if it meant he had to ride alone on an airplane. I was afraid Sophie would feel that way, too, but I knew Mom and Dad were right. I had to tell Sophie that Midnight was at my house.

I mailed my letter to Sophie the next day. I would have called her, but she had not told us her cousin's last name so I didn't know how to find a phone number. In my letter, I told her about Midnight being thrown in the Dumpster and how he shredded my stomach on the bus ride home. I told her that he and Waggy were pals, and that Midnight slept on my bed. I said my parents would pay to send him to her but that I loved him now, too, and would gladly keep him. I wanted to beg, "Please, please let me keep him," and underline it six times, but I controlled myself.

I estimated it would take two days for my letter to reach her, and two days for me to get her reply. I hoped she would answer right away.

Abby bounced into class the next morning with a big grin on her face. "I got my laptop back!" she announced. "We got everything back that had been stolen except the cash."

"Aunt Karen got her TV back, too," said Hunter, "but her other things haven't been found yet. The police think the thieves already sold them."

Mom called Mrs. Spangler to thank her for helping me. Mrs. Spangler said that a contractor was there fixing her ceiling and repairing the apartment above her.

"I'd like to visit her sometime," I said. "She doesn't get much company."

"She told me her daughter lives in Atlanta," Mom said, "and comes once a year. I think it's a fine idea for you to visit her, as long as you tell me when you want to go and let me drive you there."

"No more secret bus rides," I said. "I promise."

Luckily for my nerves, Sophie replied quickly.

Dear Emmy,

I am so happy! When I read that you have Midnight, I jumped up and down and screamed. Mama came running and when I told her and Trudy what had happened, they jumped and screamed, too. Even Cousin Joanie screamed, and she has never met Midnight.

> *We are furious with that awful man who put*
> *Midnight in the Dumpster. The day we moved out, I*
> *asked him if he had seen my cat and he said, "No." I wish*
> *Midnight had scratched him instead of you.*
>
> *Mama and I talked about your offer to send*
> *Midnight to us and I thank you for that, but I have*
> *decided that he should stay with you. I know you love him*
> *and are taking good care of him, and a long plane ride*
> *would scare him. Also, he might not get along with Joanie*
> *and Doug's two cats, and it will be a few months before*
> *we move into a home of our own. I wish I could have him*
> *back, but I think this is the best decision for Midnight. I*
> *want him to be happy.*
>
> *Tell Midnight that I love him, and I will always*
> *remember him, but he is your cat now and he should be a*
> *good boy.*
>
> *Your friend,*
> *Sophie*

As soon as I read *he should stay with you* the words on the page blurred with happy tears. When I had decided to deliver food to Sophie's family, I thought I was giving a gift to a girl in need. It turns out, she gave me a wonderful gift in return. Perhaps letting me keep Midnight was her way to thank me for collecting food when her family needed help. Or maybe she was only putting what was best for Midnight ahead of her own wishes.

I set Sophie's letter down and picked up Midnight. "You're a good cat," I said as I stroked his fur. "Sophie loves you, and I love you, too."

Midnight purred and rubbed his head against my hand.

ACKNOWLEDGMENTS

Special thanks:

To everyone at Penguin Young Reader's Group. These are smart, creative people who care about books and children; I feel fortunate to work with them. My editor, Rosanne Lauer, saw promise in my first middle-grade novel in 1986, and has helped me improve my work ever since.

To the good folks at Curtis Brown, Ltd., for their endless enthusiasm and efficiency.

Ginger Knowlton is an extraordinary agent, Dave Barbor makes sure my books are available in other languages, and Mina Feig is always way ahead of me in taking care of details.

To Pete Sheridan, Deputy Sheriff with the King County WA Sheriff's Dept., for explaining how police officers would act in my novel's circumstances.

To Chelsea Kehret for allowing me to tie her to a chair so that I could describe her efforts to get free.

To Marilyn Kamcheff for expert proofreading of the first version of this book.

To Brett Konen for insightful comments and suggestions on the final revision. Her editorial help is so valuable that I forgive her for always winning when we play Bananagrams.

To Erin Karp of Karp Business Law for making sure Dunbar's legal agreements are proper.

For more information about CaringBridge, see www.caringbridge. org.

THREE CHILLING TALES IN ONE THRILLING VOLUME FROM PEG KEHRET!

From meeting a ghost with a secret to dodging at the fair to hiding from a convict at the zoo, Ellen and Corey run into way more danger than your average kids.

FOR MORE RIVETING SUSPENSE, READ PEG KEHRET'S *ABDUCTION!*

Matt is missing. Bonnie's brother left his classroom to use the bathroom—and disappeared. Can Bonnie track him down and outsmart his abductor?